An Incident

at South

Pass

A WESTERN FRONTIER ADVENTURE

ROBERT PEECHER

For information the author may be contacted at PO Box 967; Watkinsville GA; 30677

or at rob@mooncalfpress.com

This is a work of fiction. Any similarities to actual events in whole or in part are purely accidental. None of the characters or events depicted in this novel are intended to represent actual people.

ISBN – 9798394265143

CONTENTS

1

THE TRAIL OF RUTS and hoof tracks in the sandy caliche followed a steep slope up an embankment.

The ground, hard packed when they first arrived, had broken up under the weight of the oxen and the wagons, first into clumps and then into a gritty, loose texture not hardly stiffer than the bags of sugar in the wagons. After the first score of wagons had mounted the embankment, the digging hooves of the heavy beasts had scratched the embankment so loose that the wheels wouldn't catch enough purchase to turn. Even a child walking up the embankment now felt her feet easily slip into the sand.

"We'll be all day getting these wagons over this hump," Caleb Driscoll said to Zeke Townes.

The latter wagons, another dozen after the first twenty, could only mount the embankment at a charge. And that was after the wagons had been emptied of at least the weightier bits of their load.

Caleb Driscoll, the unflappable driver who'd seen Ezekiel Townes and his family this far, was clearly the next man in line, and he gave a shout to the oxen and snapped his whip and they started to go.

Not that oxen ever went quickly. They were a lumbering beast. Nevertheless, Driscoll clearly had the right of way. His wagon was next in line, his oxen moving.

And then Marcus Weiss let out a shout.

"Belay there!" Weiss said. His deep voice and German accent gave a hint of the imperious to every phrase the man uttered. "My man is next!"

Butch Fischer, who drove for Weiss, started his team moving, even though Driscoll was already going.

The oxen of both teams were half crazed anyway. All the water since Fort Laramie was alkali and dangerous to drink, and all the livestock suffered from thirst as the emigrants rationed the water. They needed to make Sweetwater, and soon.

At the critical moment, with several men now shouting, the oxen became entangled, the leather strap of one team entwined with the yoke of the other.

The beasts bellowed and pulled against each other, and every man present saw disaster in the making.

"They'll overturn the wagon!" someone shouted, seeing Weiss's wagon make a precarious lurch up the embankment.

Several men, still waiting their turn to get their wagons up the rise, swore oaths of grievance at yet another delay. They rightfully had visions of spending all day getting a wagon upright when just a few minutes of pause might have made for a smoother passing.

"Get your man back!" Zeke Townes said angrily to Weiss.

Townes drew the big blade from its scabbard on his belt and rushed toward the ensnared animals, thinking to cut the strap. A leather strap could be replaced easier than a team of oxen or a wagon or all its contents.

A joke had gone around that Butch Fischer handled his oxen so well because his papa must've been an ox. Indeed, the resemblance was uncanny. Fischer had an expansive midsection and eyes set too wide on his head, and his bushy black beard gave an appearance like the snout of an ox.

The only part of the joke that didn't seem rooted in the truth was the assertion that Butch Fischer handled the teams well. In fact, he wasn't much of a driver at all. FIscher was a laborer, working in Weiss's gristmill back in Missouri. But there was a warrant for him in Illinois, and he'd grown tired of looking over his shoulder. When Weiss announced that he was selling his mill and bound for the Oregon Territory, Fischer offered his services as driver. He'd drive the team for wages and work for Weiss's new venture in Oregon. All he knew of driving a team of oxen, though, was brute force and foul language, both of which he employed liberally.

"You dadburn cows!" Fischer shouted, and he brought his whip down with such force upon the hide of one of Townes's team that the ox bucked and kicked.

"Careful there!" Caleb Driscoll yelled. "You're making it worse!"

"I'll make you worse!" Butch Fischer shouted, and now brought down his whip again, lashing Driscoll across the face so that the man reeled as if punched by a heavy blow, and a welt immediately appeared, stained crimson.

A woman shrieked at the sight of the violence.

Several men started forward, sensing disaster at the door. Among them came Zeke Townes, his exposed knife already gripped in his fist.

Fischer saw the knife and thought Townes intended violence.

"Come armed at me, you cur dog!" Fischer shouted, and he lashed the whip at Zeke Townes, catching him across the face.

Caleb Driscoll, already a victim of Fischer's whip, now charged forward, even as Townes righted himself.

Fischer gave Driscoll a lash, and then another. Zeke Townes reached the big man and grabbed the wrist of his whip hand and tried to stop him. But Fischer's girth gave him quite a bit of strength, and his heavy arm pushed down against Townes, shaking the man off. Driscoll bashed Townes in the head with the grip of the whip, cutting a gash in Townes's forehead from which blood ran freely.

Some would say it was a deliberate act in revenge for the whipping. Others claimed it looked to them like an accident.

For his own part, Zeke Townes swore he never intended it.

But whatever the intention, as Fischer raised up his arm to bring the whip down on Zeke Townes again, Townes thrust forward with the knife, catching Fischer in the side just below his armpit.

2

"Murder!" Marcus Weiss shouted.

Zeke Townes backed away. His mouth hanging open.

Butch Fischer backed away, his right arm raised into the air, the knife sticking out of his side. A woman standing below on the embankment let loose a terrible scream, as if she'd just witnessed a massacre and might be the next victim.

"What have you done?" Fischer demanded, his arm hanging over his head, his head strained forward so that he could see the grip of the knife stuck in him. "What have you done?"

Zeke Townes went mute, unable to form words. He stood aghast against what had transpired, unable to even conceive of how his knife had gone into Fischer's side. Worse, he'd run the knife all the way to the hilt.

Butch Fischer shouted an agonized howl of pain as he reached up with his left arm, gripped the knife, and gave it an almighty wrench to pull it loose.

Fischer swooned and dropped the knife. He fell to one knee, reaching out with his left hand to catch himself, his right hand still hanging above his head, exposing the sight of the wound. And a ghastly sight it was. The moment he'd pulled the knife away, the blood ran freely, ferociously, pouring out of him like it had been turned loose from a spout. Fischer went faint and fell back on the ground. He made a wail, a mixture of pain and sorrow.

He tried to speak, but no clear words came.

Marcus Weiss, closest to him now, stood by and did nothing. Caleb Driscoll, though, did rush to the man's aid, pulling his own shirt from his back, wadding it, and pressing it against Fischer's wound. The shirt quickly went from a dirty white to red.

Having traveled some six hundred miles or more together, they knew that Lillian Marsh was the closest thing to a doctor in the party, and someone had the presence of mind now to rush forward and call her back. The wife of a preacher who intended to start a mission to the natives, Mrs. Marsh had ministered to the party's physical ailments while her husband tended to their spiritual needs. She had relieved headaches with powders, cleaned and bandaged nicks and scrapes, stitched a bad gash on Willie Burmeister's leg, and even set a broken arm.

But by the time she arrived at the embankment, she found Butch Fischer in a state where she could do nothing for him.

No one had been able to stop the flow of blood, and she could find neither pulse nor breath.

"I am sorry to say that Mr. Fischer is quite beyond my abilities," Mrs. Marsh said sadly. "Among our party, only my husband can intercede on his behalf now."

In the wake of the violence which had taken place, some of the other men nearby came and cut the straps on Weiss's team to free the oxen. A few put their backs into the wagon while others worked the team, and they pushed Weiss's wagon up the embankment, past the body of the man who had recently driven the team.

By now, the wagons forward had come to a halt and all in the party were aware that some incident had transpired near the back.

Elias Townes and some of the other men made the trek to the rear to see about the issue.

Elias Townes stood close to six feet. He had broad shoulders and long legs, and he'd put those legs to good use. The men in the party teased that Elias should have been at the rear because with his stride he set too fast a pace for the oxen to keep up. They teased that if Elias had walked on ahead alone, without oxen or wagons or women and children to slow him, he'd be to the Pacific Ocean by now. But when it came time back in Independence to elect a leader, it was Elias Townes they chose. He was approaching thirty-five years in age, and of the more than one hundred souls in the wagon train, now known as the Townes Party, a fair number were of some relation. Zeke Townes was his younger brother. Elias's eldest daughter, Maggie, at seventeen, had just married Jason Winter, and they had joined the expedition west. Elias Townes also brought his wife Madeline and their four younger children, the boys Gabriel and Christian and the two younger girls Martha and Mary.

Caleb Driscoll worked for Elias Townes and his brother Zeke, as did a number of the men driving the wagons and the livestock belonging to the Townes family.

"What's happened here?" Elias Townes demanded as he worked his way down the embankment. A large crowd, perhaps thirty or more women, children, and men, had gathered.

Elias directed his question to the shirtless Caleb Driscoll, who also bore a terrible welt on his face, but even as Elias Townes asked the question, he saw the body in the sandy dirt alongside the trail, saw the stained shirt that was used to try to staunch the blood. And then his eyes fell on the weapon used to take the man's life. The bloody knife. Elias recognized the knife, for it had been a gift he'd presented to his younger brother at the journey's beginning.

"Zeke?" Elias called, looking among the crowd that had gathered, but he did not see his little brother.

"He's over behind the wagon there," Caleb Driscoll said, nodding his head at Zeke Townes's wagon. "Marie is seeing to his injuries."

"Injuries?" Elias questioned.

"Yes, sir," Caleb said. He nodded his head now to the body on the ground. "It was Butch Fischer's fault, there. I started Mr. Zeke's team up the embankment here, and Fischer charged ahead, trying to beat us up the rise. The oxes got tangled there, and we looked to have a real mess on our hands."

Marcus Weiss was huddled with a couple of men nearby. He'd been stating his case, blaming the entire incident on Driscoll and Zeke Townes. Weiss now raised up a hand and took several steps toward Elias.

"I told you to give way!" Marcus said, directing his comment toward Caleb Driscoll.

"We was next in line!" Caleb said, shouting right back at the man.

Zeke Townes, upon hearing the fresh round of quarreling, came around the side of his wagon. His face covered in blood, and a wound on his forehead.

"Stand down, Caleb!" Zeke called.

Then the younger Townes man saw his brother.

"Zeke? What happened?" Elias asked.

"The teams got tangled – my team and Mr. Weiss's. I intended to cut them free before we had some calamity. But Weiss's driver, Fischer, he started coming at Caleb and then at me with his whip."

Ezekiel Townes shook his head slowly and closed his eyes as he tried to picture in his mind all that had transpired. Anyone could see the turmoil on his face.

"I don't know, Elias," Zeke said. "I don't know how it happened. I had the knife in my hand to cut the team loose, and then Fischer assaulted me with the whip, and I stabbed him."

"Killed him is what you did!" Marcus Weiss interjected. "He's killed my teamster!"

Zeke frowned, his eyes almost pleading as he looked at his brother. But he nodded his head.

"I did," Zeke said. "I killed the man."

Elias Townes never sought to be in charge of the wagon train. He was promoted by others and elected at-large. But he'd taken the responsibility foisted upon him, making his priority the welfare of every man, woman, and child in his charge. He'd settled mild disputes, he'd sought aid for people who had lost supplies or livestock, he'd reached into his own pocket more than once to cover debts incurred at forts along the way so that one pioneer in the train did not owe another who refused to wait for payment. A thousand little decisions came his way, nuisances he'd rather have done without. But he'd accepted them and dealt with them.

But murder – now this was something new, made doubly difficult that his own brother stood accused.

Elias sighed heavily as he looked at young Zeke, and he shook his head sorrowfully. He did not know what he was to do.

"Hang him!" Marcus Weiss demanded. "I'll not travel another foot with a murderer. Nor will I see this wagon train move an inch without justice. Hang him!"

From the moment they'd ferried the wagons over the Missouri, Marcus Weiss became an irritant among the party.

He complained incessantly. He picked quarrels with others in the wagon train. Daily, he abused Elias Townes with questions to which Elias did not know the answers. He wanted to know the distance to the next fork or the next landmark and how many days it would take. He endeavored to keep a daily accounting of the journey, and so he wanted precise information as to how far they'd traveled in a day. When the party came upon a stream, Weiss would ride ahead to the front to seek out Elias Townes and ask the name of the stream.

The second day after arriving at the Platte, the party came upon an Indian burial site. From the scaffold on which the body was interred, Weiss took a large necklace of some sort made of bone and adorned with feathers.

Several people complained. They said he would incur the wrath of the Tribes and lead to ruin for all of them. Most among the party feared Indian attack above all else, and some had even objected to crossing alongside the burial site, preferring instead to go some distance away. Others, more superstitious in nature, thought Weiss might bring upon them "bad medicine." They feared supernatural retribution for the theft.

And perhaps worst of all, there was the business with his wife. Weiss had showed himself to be a cruel bully toward the woman, and not a soul in the party failed to take notice.

His driver, Butch Fischer, was a mean-spirited man. If anything, his temperament was worse than that of his employer. Now, with

Fischer dead on the ground and Weiss demanding justice by hanging, it came as no surprise to Elias Townes that Weiss and Fischer caused the first significant test of his leadership.

"We'll go no farther today," Elias said. "Spread the word to the other wagons. Circle them up ahead. Unburden your teams, make your camps."

"It's not yet noontime," someone argued. "We're giving up half a day's travel."

"We've only made about three miles from last night's camp," some other man complained. "I think I can see the spot where we camped last night on the horizon, yonder."

But the complaints fell on deaf ears. Elias had made the decision.

"We'll circle up the wagons that are already over the embankment," Elias said. "The ones at the rear should be brought up over the embankment so that in the morning we'll be able to get started without delay."

He issued his orders with an expectation that those within earshot would share the information with those ahead or behind.

Elias formed a tribunal, as he might have done had he been at the head of some military expedition.

He selected Captain Walker, a veteran of the Seminole Wars, who had witnessed the incident, or at least some part of it. He also chose Reverend Marsh. The three of them together would sit in judgment of Elias's brother. He believed both men possessed intellect and sound reason; but most of all, Elias believed that they were Christian men, charitable and merciful. That was the best he could do to put a thumb on the scales of justice for his brother's benefit.

The three men walked together to the front of the train, to where Elias Townes's family waited to hear of what had transpired at the rear. But they were disappointed, for Elias did not share with them the news. Instead, he told his sons and his hired driver to turn the wagons and then to release the oxen and make camp. Those wagons that had already cleared the embankment were brought forward into a circle, smaller than usual for the absence of the wagons still behind the embankment, but still large enough to serve as a corral for the livestock.

The three men took chairs away from the others, and they sat on the open prairie to deliberate.

"The facts are not in dispute," Elias said.

"Let me start by saying that I witnessed some portion of the transaction, and I'll not allow them to hang your brother," Captain Walker said. "That man Fischer, a known brute, was thrashing your brother with his whip handle. Your brother struck in self-defense."

Elias looked to Reverend Marsh to see how he took this. The preacher nodded his head thoughtfully.

"Indeed," he said. "From the little I was able to discern, I agree that it sounds as if Mr. Townes acted in self-defense. However, he did come forward with a knife."

"To cut away the tangled strap," Walker interjected.

"Perhaps," the preacher said with a small shrug. "No one can say what was in Ezekiel's heart when he approached Mr. Fischer. And none can dispute that at this very moment a party of men is digging a grave for Mr. Fischer. It's an unfortunate incident."

Not unexpectedly, Marcus Weiss now approached the tribunal, marching with high steps that suggested he was already anticipating an argument. They ceased their deliberations as they watched him approach.

"I'll be heard on this matter," Weiss said, standing in front of the three seated men.

"Have your say, Mr. Weiss," Elias said.

"Justice demands your brother be hanged for the murder of my man Fischer," Weiss said. "This incident could have readily been resolved, but Townes stormed forward, knife in hand, to force violence where none need occur. If you fail to give justice here, I'll have the three of you arrested, along with Ezekiel Townes, when we arrive at the next fort."

"Have us arrested?" Captain Walker said with a scoff. "On what charge?"

"Assisting in murder!" Marcus Weiss barked.

"You'll not threaten me, Weiss!" Captain Walker said, and he started to rise, but Reverend Marsh put out a hand and patted the captain on his thigh. Walker resumed his seat, a scowl writ deeply across his face.

"It's a long way to the Oregon Territory, Mr. Weiss," Reverend Marsh said gently. "If you intend to make the entire journey with this party, I might recommend a conciliatory posture."

"Conciliatory?" Weiss demanded. "Ezekiel Townes killed my hired driver. I'll not be conciliatory. It was murder, and the punishment for murder is to hang."

"I witnessed what occurred, and it was self-defense," Captain Walker said.

"No such thing!" Weiss said. "Mr. Fischer did not even render the man unconscious. How can anyone claim the killing was done in self-defense when the only injury sustained by Mr. Townes was a slight knock to the head?"

"Nothing slight about it," Walker said. "The man's seeing his injuries tended to now."

Even as Weiss made his angry argument, a small delegation, self-appointed and unbidden, approached the tribunal. They'd appointed Jefferson Pilcher as their spokesman, or, at the least, it was

Pilcher who now addressed the tribunal on their behalf. As they made their way to the three seated judges, Weiss stepped aside, allowing them to have their say.

"Elias, you know I've got no quarrel with your brother. I've driven my wagon just behind his for all this way so far, and he's helped me to no end. But we thought you should know that several of the women who witnessed the – how to put it? – the killing. Several of the women have said they'll not continue forward in Zeke's presence."

Another of the men cut in.

"We all like Zeke," he said. "He's the first in this party to throw a shoulder into the back of a stuck wagon, and Lord knows we can use his strength at the difficult parts. But the women – they're making a lot of noise."

"The women who witnessed the assault!" Weiss spoke up. "Do their concerns count for nothing? A man is murdered, and the witnesses won't travel with the guilty party. Nothing more needs to be said other than to issue the order to fetch a rope!"

Pilcher made a face at Weiss, and he seemed uncomfortable with his part in the discussion.

"We all say it's self-defense," Pilcher said. "And none of us would stand to see him hanged. But what we're saying is, Zeke needs to be cut loose from the party."

"Banishment?" Elias demanded. "Banishment is your answer? That's as much a death sentence as hanging him outright!"

"Banishment would satisfy justice!" Weiss declared.

Pilcher turned his back on the tribunal. He'd said what he'd come to say, and not believing it just himself, he could add no more. His wife, and some of the other women, they'd been adamant. Some wanted Weiss also banished, though the men couldn't even devise an argument in favor of that. Weiss had committed no injury in the altercation.

It came as no surprise to Pilcher, who had camped near to Marcus Weiss, that some of the women sought to see him banished as well. There'd been cruel sounds coming from the Weiss camp on more than one night. Word had spread quickly through the Townes party that Marcus Weiss abused his wife, perhaps on an almost daily basis. But a husband's treatment of his wife was considered to be a matter between the husband and the wife. Perhaps her family, if her father or brothers had been present, might intervene. But strangers traveling in the same wagon train – it wasn't their place.

Only Zeke Townes had intervened, doing so through a private conversation with Weiss. None were present but the two men, but Pilcher had heard that Zeke Townes offered to give Weiss the same treatment if he did not leave off the beatings.

Elias Townes let out a heavy sigh. Others were coming from the camp now.

He wanted a private conversation with Reverend Marsh and Captain Walker. He wanted the three of them to deliberate and reach a conclusion. Elias had it in mind that they might shackle Zeke during the nights and that might satisfy the others in the party, but instead, Pilcher and the others were pushing for banishment.

Elias already had made up his mind that if it came to it, he would never sentence his own brother to death – not for an act that could reasonably be viewed as self-defense.

But in the interest of justice, Elias had also decided, even before the tribunal first took its seats, that whichever man offered the harshest sentence short of hanging, Elias would agree with that man. It was right and proper to do so. Whatever obligation he had to his own brother, he also had a duty to the wagon train. They had elected him to do a job – keep the peace among the pioneers and get as many of them as possible safely to the Oregon Territory.

Elias had hoped that both men might rule Zeke as innocent of murder. In that case, he could in good conscience vote with them. But if one or the other came down on the side of punishment – whatever punishment – Elias would go with that. And if both Marsch and Walker said it should be hanging for Zeke, Zeke would be hanged but with Elias objecting.

Caleb Driscoll pressed a cloth against his injured face. He'd put on a shirt by now. He was at the front of a fresh group coming from the wagons. There were women, too, among the crowd. Elias recognized Pilcher's wife. He did not see his family – neither his wife nor his son-in-law, none of his children, and not Ezekiel or Zeke's wife, Marie.

"I've come to say that anything Mr. Zeke did, he did it on my behalf," Driscoll said the moment he was in earshot, still walking toward the three seated men and their growing audience. "If you intend to hang Mr. Zeke, you'll have to hang me right alongside of him."

"He won't be hanged, Mr. Driscoll," Captain Walker said, and he stood up from his chair as he said it. "I'll shoot any man who goes for a rope."

"He murdered my teamster!" Weiss said.

"Everyone calm down," Elias Townes said, also standing up. He envisioned the tribunal devolving into an open brawl with both Driscoll and Weiss there.

Elias Townes first hired Caleb Driscoll when the boy was about twelve years old.

Elias had owned a timber lease and sawmill back in Kentucky. More than a year back, Elias and his youngest brother, Ezekiel, had talked of taking the Oregon Trail. Quickly, the talk went from idle chat to serious planning. And when Elias sold his business, he hired on his best men to make the trip west. Driscoll was one of the first they approached.

The Townes brothers intended to set up a new sawmill in Oregon. They had a half dozen hard working men and several wagons of tools and supplies. They envisioned a time when they turned to construction, maybe building entire towns from the boards cut at their mill.

Caleb was just a mite younger than Zeke, and the two had all but grown up together. They'd been the best of pals, and Caleb's devotion to Zeke came as no surprise.

"None of the facts are in dispute," Elias said. "The three of us will reach a conclusion, and we do not need any further assistance."

"Who will drive my team?" Weiss demanded.

"I'll send my son Gabriel, and he can drive your team," Elias Townes said. Gabe, though perhaps a little young to drive a team on the two-thousand mile overland route, had been driving wagons from when he was small enough to sit on his father's knee and hold the lines. Gabe had already driven one of his father's wagons much of the way on this journey, though his primary responsibility was to join the other drovers in keeping the livestock.

"I'll not have it," Weiss said. "I'll not trade a good and competent driver for a boy."

None could argue that the man deserved to be compensated for the loss of his driver. Any of them would have expected the same.

"I'll drive the Weiss team," Caleb Driscoll spoke up. "You can send Gabe back to drive Mr. Zeke's team."

"You're a good man, Caleb," Elias Townes said. "That's settled then, Mr. Weiss. You have a driver for your team."

"That satisfies the loss of my driver," Weiss said. "But what of justice, Mr. Townes? What justice will we have for this murder? The man deserves to be hanged, whether he is your brother or not."

"The women," Jefferson Pilcher said. "I've told you what they have said about traveling with a man who has committed murder. You should consider that, Elias."

Pilcher didn't seem to take any pleasure in the reminding, but that last statement felt like a warning. Would there be a revolt if Elias Townes did not banish his brother?

Another question that plagued Elias, one he had no time to fully consider: Would it be so bad if there was a revolt?

Between Elias Townes's wagons and hired men, and Zeke's wagons and hired men, and the wagon belonging to Jason Winter, Elias's son-in-law, the Townes family brought a significant portion of the wagon train. If the train split, there would certainly be those who would go with the Towneses. Elias could put it to them plainly – his brother acted in self-defense and he would not be sending off his own flesh and blood for such a thing. Those who didn't like it were free to go on their own.

A wry grin crossed Elias's face now as he thought that they could elect Marcus Weiss as their new leader.

But Elias also had full faith in his own abilities. On a trail where every mile threatened to claim a life, Elias believed he could get the most of their party safely along the route. And so, like it or not, he was bound by the duty given him to keep this party together, at least as far as Bridger's Fort, and keep his charges alive.

"I'll discuss this no further with anyone outside of the tribunal," Elias said.

He and Captain Walker both resumed their seats, and the three men huddled together.

The crowd that had gathered showed deference to the judges and milled about beyond earshot. Most spoke to each other about the sorry circumstances. Caleb Driscoll stood aloof, unwilling to speak or be spoken to and disinterested in anything except the tribunal's decision. Marcus Weiss crossed his arms, flung back his shoulders, and stood imperious, watching the others who were all unwilling to speak to him.

"We should find that your brother acted in self-defense and conclude these proceedings," Captain Walker said. "The sooner the better. By God! We've seen already more dissension in our ranks than I'd have ever tolerated among my men fighting the Indians. It won't do to have more."

Elias breathed a small sigh of relief. He would vote the same if Reverend Marsh would also agree.

But for several long moments, the preacher sat silently in contemplation. When he at last broke his silence, Elias could not have been more disappointed.

"The Old Testament tells us that a man who sheds blood should have his blood shed by man," Reverend Marsh said. "But Jesus brought a new covenant. Did He not? But did not Paul tell the Romans to not repay evil with evil? I am convicted that a hanging would be compounding evil. But Paul also said to the Romans to do what is honorable in the eyes of all. I daresay, releasing young Mr. Townes as if nothing has happened would be dishonorable in the eyes of some."

The man seemed to be giving voice to his private meditations on the issue, and neither Captain Walker nor Elias were inclined to interrupt.

"The offspring of the righteous shall be delivered," Reverend Marsh said.

He took a deep breath and then began to nod his head as if he had reached a conclusion.

"My vote is for banishment," he said. "Send him away. If he is innocent in the eyes of the Lord, no harm will come to him. He will pass safely back to Fort Laramie."

"Would you also send away the man's wife and child to die on the prairie?" Captain Walker snarled.

"Of course not," Reverend Marsh said. "But it's clear from what Mr. Pilcher said that Ezekiel cannot remain with the wagon train. If it is God's will, he will safely return to Fort Laramie. He can winter there. And in the spring, he can join a train headed west to reunite with his family."

"I won't agree to that," Captain Walker said. "He's one of the most able men in our company. We need him here, and these women be damned."

"Please, Captain Walker!" Reverend Marsh reprimanded.

Elias took a heavy breath and pursed his lips so hard that they began to turn white.

"You'll not be moved from your position, Reverend?" Elias said.

"I think not," Marsh said. "I am satisfied that this is the honorable way. Banishment puts justice in God's hands. For my part, I will pray for young Zeke's safe arrival back at Fort Laramie."

Elias nodded.

"I thank you both for your assistance," Elias said.

Walker looked up sharply.

"That's a decision made, then?" the captain asked.

"It is," Elias said.

"Self-defense?" Captain Walker asked, almost pleading.

Elias stood up, his head hung so low that his chin nearly touched his chest.

"Please be good enough to take my chair back to my wagon?" Elias said to Captain Walker. "I need to go and tell my brother our decision so that he can begin to make his arrangements."

3

MARIE LECOINTRE WAS BORN in New Orleans in 1826.

Her grandparents on her father's side of the family fled France during the country's Revolution, coming to what was then Spanish-held New Orleans. Her mother's family was already there, having been part of the early French community that helped to settle New Orleans. When she was still a young girl, her father took his family up the Mississippi River, settling in the burgeoning city of St. Louis, originally a French community and still with enough French influence that the Lecointre family felt plenty at home.

But when Marie was still young, her father moved the family to Paducah, Kentucky, a growing hub of the river shipping business. It was there that Marie met the young Ezekiel Townes. The Townes family was already prominent in the Paducah area. They owned a gristmill and a farm, and the family's oldest son owned a prosperous sawmill.

They met as children, Marie Lecointre and Ezekiel Townes. Their homes were not much farther than a rock's throw from each other. As small children, they played in creeks together. As they got older, Zeke's interest in the pretty, dark-haired French girl grew to something different.

To Zeke, Marie was very French in appearance, and foreign in some of her mannerisms. Her face, framed by dark brown hair, featured a long but thin nose and large hazel eyes that sometimes turned green when she was very excited. The slight accent to her speech, adopted from her parents who spoke French in the home, gave her an enchanting aura. Even as a young boy, when stomping together through mud holes was the only ritual of courtship he understood, Zeke intuitively knew that Marie Lecointre was his woman and he was her man.

For her part, Marie never doubted the inevitability of the relationship. Even when her father made a mild attempt at forbidding the relationship – "He is not Catholic, nor even French," was her father's complaint – Marie still often started statements to Zeke: "When we are wed."

"It's a terrible gash," Marie said now, pulling away the blood-matted hair to try to get a look at her husband's injury.

"Don't dig at it so hard," Zeke winced.

"I am only pushing the hair aside."

"Well, push gentler."

She took a wet cloth and dabbed at the wound and the blood in the hair and tried to clean it. They were at the back of their wagon, Zeke seated on a chair. A wagon train afforded little privacy, and a few of those who'd been at the front of the train and had not seen the incident came back now to see what had happened. Women and children, mostly, as the men were seeing to their wagons.

Seeing that the injury needed to be stitched, Marie asked one of the nearby children to go and ask for Mrs. Marsh who was a hand at such things.

"What will they do to you?" Marie asked, still cleaning her husband's hair.

"I don't know," Zeke said. "I didn't mean to kill that man."

"I know you did not," Marie said.

"He was hittin' me with that whip handle, and I just tried to stop him."

Marie grinned ruefully. She'd always had a vicious sense of humor.

"I would say that you succeeded," she muttered, careful not to allow any of the onlookers to overhear.

"I reckon I did," Zeke said, chuckling a bit. He took no joy in killing Butch Fischer, but neither was Zeke the sort to lament too long over a bad situation.

They were quiet for a moment, except for Zeke wincing and sucking air as Marie touched his injured head.

He still felt a bit dazed, but his senses were together enough to know that the next hour or so might hold bad news for him.

"They might decide to hang me," Zeke said.

"They wouldn't!" Marie gasped.

"They might," Zeke said. "If they do, you go on to Oregon with Elias. He'll see to your needs, and he'll raise Daniel up to be a good man."

At the mention of their three-year-old son, Marie's eyes involuntarily shot up and scanned the horizon. He was there with some of his cousins watching over him, out in the prairie grass. Such was the life of an emigrant mother – constantly worrying over where her child was and what he might have gotten into.

"Elias wouldn't hang you," Marie said.

"Probably not," Zeke said, trying to think clearly despite the throbbing in his head. "But they might also banish me."

"No," Marie breathed. She didn't need to be told what banishment meant. A lone man on this empty prairie – if he didn't fall prey to the Savages, then surely starvation would get him, or he would die of thirst. The horrors of being alone on the prairie were too much to consider. Banishment was perhaps worse than hanging him outright because banishment almost certainly brought on a slow, lingering death. At least a hanging ended quickly.

"Whatever happens, if I ain't here to see to you and Daniel, you carry on with Elias. And don't harbor ill will against him. Whatever he does, he'll do it because he thinks it's best. You can't fault him for it."

The two of them remained silent for a moment. Marie held the damp cloth to her husband's head, and she watched her son playing in the tall grass with Elias's two younger daughters. The older one, a Winter now, but still every bit a Townes, watched over the children. Elias's daughters all treated Daniel like a younger brother, doting on him and mothering him until he could no longer stand it and would run to find his father. He idolized Elias's sons, Gabe and Christian, followed them like a puppy.

"He will not send you away," Marie said.

"It won't be up to him, not entirely," Zeke said. "He called together a tribunal."

"Not with that Marcus Weiss!" Marie hissed.

"No. Of course not. Captain Walker and Reverend Marsh are the other two."

At the mention of her husband's name, Lillian Marsh cleared her throat. She'd just walked up.

"Do you want me to look at the injury?" Mrs. Marsh said.

She had with her a little leather bag that people had taken to calling her doctor's bag.

"Please," Marie said.

Marie stepped back, giving Mrs. Marsh room to work. She had the cloth in her hand still and saw the moist blood on it. She dipped the cloth in water and rung it out. A group of men had walked some ways off the trail with shovels and had started digging a grave for Butch Fischer. Marie felt no sympathy for the man. He was coarse and rude. Several times around their camps, Marie had caught Fischer watching her, and she did not like his lustful stares. She had not mentioned them to her husband, but she found herself always staying aware of Fischer's location around camp so as to avoid him. She'd feared any occasion where she might be away from camp – cleaning dishes in a stream or relieving herself – and encounter him, and she always made certain to have a knife with her whenever she walked away by herself.

So she did not mourn this man or have any sympathy for him. If he'd had a family, it might be different.

But she did not believe she would mourn Weiss, either, if some tragedy befell him, and he had a family.

4

—— ◆ ——

THE TWO BROTHERS STOOD on a high hill overlooking the train of wagons, most circled to create a corral to keep the livestock, others dotting away from the circle and down toward Zeke Townes's wagon which, for the moment, sat last in line.

"I'm sorry to put you to this trouble," Zeke said.

"It's yourself you've put to trouble," Elias told him. They'd walked together in silence until reaching the hilltop, and then Elias stopped but still did not speak for some time.

"What's my fate?" Zeke said.

"Banishment," Elias said. "I didn't have any choice, none that I saw. Some of the women said they wouldn't go on with you, and Marcus Weiss wanted to see you hanged."

"Good luck finding a tree from which to do it," Zeke said bitterly.

Elias grinned.

"There's some cottonwoods down along the river," he said. His eyes swept the landscape in front of them. "That pine yonder, that might have some stout enough branches up high. We could toss a rope over."

Zeke tried to muster a smile at the joke but couldn't do it. Elias kept his eyes on the ground, only glancing at his brother, unable to look him in the eye.

"Captain Walker wanted to let you go free. Reverend Marsh seemed to take into account the will of the women in the train. Some of them said they wouldn't go on with a man who has taken a life. Marsh said banishment, and I felt a duty to the people who elected me their leader to go along with the preacher. I figured to counterweigh my own bias, I must side with whichever man offered the harshest punishment short of hanging, which I could not concede. So, it's banishment," Elias said. "I'm sorry, brother."

Zeke shook his head ruefully.

"Elias, you might as well hang me. A lone man here in the wilderness – it's a death sentence."

"Marcus Weiss certainly seems to think so," Elias said. He was unable to look his younger brother in the eye through the entirety of the conversation. He kept his eyes firmly fixed on the ground. "He wanted you hanged, but he was quick enough to settle for banishment."

"I'm sure he was," Zeke said.

"You can turn around and go back," Elias suggested. "Maybe there's a wagon train behind us that you could join on with. Trouble is, there may not be one. We got such a late start in the season, we may be the last train out this year."

That problem had cursed them all through the journey.

Late snows delayed them leaving Paducah. When they finally arrived at Independence, all the reliable and experienced wagon train captains had been hired and had started west. Those who remained and offered their services were unfit, in Elias's estimation. Zeke had agreed with him. They seemed grifters or drunks, or both. One or two of them struck Elias as outright criminals, men who would possibly get them out on the open prairie only to rob them or refuse to go farther without additional payment beyond previous agreements.

But over the course of a week, as Elias sought a captain to lead their wagon train, he encountered several people who also hoped to leave Independence while there was time. Eventually, the company grew. Several men – Captain Walker, Elias Townes, Jefferson Pilcher, even Marcus Weiss – had agreed to give it a go without hiring a wagon train captain. They'd been told that they could follow the trail of the wagons ahead without any difficulty and that enterprising men could make the journey even without benefit of an experienced leader.

Elias and Zeke, with the combination of their own hired men, could not think of anyone more enterprising than themselves.

They did hire a young man, Henry Blair, who had made the trip west as a trapper a couple of years previous. He'd never been farther west than Bridger's Fort, and he said he wouldn't lead them nor be responsible, but for the opportunity to go with the wagon train and for a little pay, he would drive the livestock, offer his advice and assistance on traversing rivers and cliffs and some of the other natural obstacles, and put his back into any work that needed doing.

And so they set out. Immediately, though, there were disputes on the order of march and arguments over livestock, and the entire enterprise seemed likely to breakdown almost within sight of Fort Leavenworth.

That was when they elected Elias as their captain.

A late start also meant that parts of the trail were bogged down where the wagons ahead had churned soil to mush.

At Fort Laramie they learned that there was a wagon train about four days ahead of them, and Elias still hoped to catch that train by the time they arrived at Bridger's Fort. The roughest, least known part of the journey would come beyond Bridger's Fort, and Elias hoped to be within sight of another train when they encountered that territory.

"It's eighty miles or so back to Fort Laramie," Elias said from the hilltop where he delivered to his brother the verdict.

They'd spent two days camping at Fort Laramie, resupplying and making repairs to damaged wagons, preparing the wagon train for the next part of the journey that would see them through some rough countryside. From the brief stay at Fort Laramie, Elias knew that Zeke could find work at the fort, and a room. The fort would offer protection from Indian attack, should a thing like that happen, and would also provide shelter through the winter.

"If there's not a wagon train behind us that you can join up with, you can winter at the fort. Come on to Oregon City in the spring with the first of next year's trains. Take Marie and Daniel back with you if you want."

"I won't risk my family alone on the prairie," Zeke said.

"Then saddle your horse and pack a second horse, and you can tote supplies enough to make eighty miles."

Zeke shook his head.

"I didn't come so far to turn back," Zeke said. "You know me well enough to know for yourself that I ain't a go-back."

Elias nodded his head. Zeke was still a young man and lacked patience. A month seemed a vast amount of time, but waiting eight or nine months for the next season of wagon trains – why, that might as well be an eternity to a young man, especially a young man separated from his family.

"I didn't figure you would want to go back," Elias said. "From the map I have, I reckon Fort Bridger is maybe three hundred miles ahead of us. You might go on ahead of us, travel fast and light, and make it to the fort. Maybe at Bridger's you can catch the wagon train ahead of us and join on with them. They can get you to Oregon City. If they're already gone, you'll have to winter at Fort Bridger. But if you like the look of the place, and you want, Marie and Daniel can winter with you there. Then all of you come on in the spring with the first wagon train you can get on with. If you don't want to keep them at the fort for the winter, then they can continue with us and you come when you can."

Zeke nodded his head.

"That's a possibility," he said, feeling some sense of relief. "I can make it three hundred miles."

"It'll take us most of a month to make it to Bridger's Fort, but on horseback, you could be there in a week or so. Like I said, if you like what you see, when we catch up to you, you can keep Marie and Daniel with you. Or, they can come on with us and be waiting for you in the territory next summer. You know I'll see after them."

Zeke glanced at the sky overhead. Still plenty of daylight for him to ride out. It seemed unreal to think of it, like this was a dream or something he was watching happen to someone else. He'd taken another man's life, and now – banished from the wagon train! He couldn't believe this was even happening to him. In his mind, he labored over the events that led to his stabbing Butch Fischer. He couldn't recall actually striking out with the knife. The moment was such chaos. That brute was beating him with the whip handle, and Zeke only thought to protect himself, never to kill.

"I sure didn't mean to put you in this position," Zeke said.

"I know you didn't," Elias said. "Bend your head, let me see it."

Zeke plucked his hat from his head and leaned forward so that Elias could see the injury. It was cleaned up, and Mrs. Marsh had put sutures in it to hold it all together.

"He gave you a mighty smart lick, though. Didn't he?" Elias said.

"He did indeed."

"You paid it back to him, though," Elias said.

"I didn't do it on purpose. I just meant to stop him from hitting me."

"I understand," Elias said. "I'd have done the same in your position. Anyone would have."

Zeke took a heavy breath. He wasn't sure that he felt any better about his fate, but he knew he had to march into it with confidence that he'd survive. Three hundred miles to Bridger's Fort. He could make that, he told himself, so long as he didn't run into hostile Indians. And then it was a new question – would he find another wagon train to travel with or would he have to wait until spring?

"I'll leave out this afternoon. I'll saddle Duke and pack one of the other horses. If I leave now, I might can make it ahead to the fort before the train ahead of us leaves."

"I'm going to walk back to my wagon," Elias said. "Don't leave without seeing me again."

"It's to be banishment," Ezekiel told his wife as he returned to the wagon, intending to make a short goodbye.

"No," Marie said, and she threw her arms around him and pressed her face against his shoulder. "They cannot do this to you."

"Everything will be fine," Zeke said. "There's a fort ahead, not three hundred miles from here. I'm going to pack a horse and take Duke and ride on ahead. I'll get to the fort ahead of you and see what arrangements I can make. If I can find another train going to

Oregon, I will try to join it. If there is any way, when you and Daniel reach the fort, you can join me in that train. If I cannot wait for you, then I'll go on ahead of you and meet you in Oregon City."

"What if there is no train you can join?" Marie asked.

"Then you and Daniel will go on without me. I will winter at the fort and wait for a wagon train next spring. I'll join you in Oregon City come summer."

Marie envisioned the next three or four months, making what remained of the journey without her husband, a man who had been by her side almost as long as she could remember, ever since she was a child.

"We will go with you," she said.

Zeke shook his head.

"No. A lone wagon on the prairie becomes a target, either for Indians or outlaws," Zeke said. "I won't put you in that kind of danger."

"And what of a lone rider?" Marie said.

"A lone man on horseback can avoid trouble," Zeke said confidently, whether he felt that confidence or not.

"And who will be there if some accident befalls you?"

"There will be no accident," Zeke said, shushing her concerns. "You're worrying over phantoms."

"I do not want to go without you," Marie said. "If you must winter at the fort, Daniel and I will winter at the fort as well."

"You may not have a choice," Zeke told her, and he stepped back to where he could look her in the eyes and he held her shoulders firmly, trying to impose on her the resolve he wanted to feel for himself. "What happened today – it wasn't what I wanted. I never intended to kill that man. But I did what I did, and there's no changing that now. And sending me away? It's what Elias has to do. I hold no ill will toward him. You understand?"

"I understand," Marie said, blinking her moist, hazel eyes at him.

"Elias will take care of you. Whether he has to do it to the next fort or all the way to Oregon. And one way or another, we'll be together again in Oregon. Sooner or later. But you must listen to me, because we do not have much time before I have to leave. As I go on ahead, I'll leave messages for you so that you know I am still with you. If I can get on with another train at the fort, I'll do that. If I cannot wait for you – if I have to move on with another wagon train – I'll leave word for you. Rely on Elias and Caleb Driscoll. They'll get you as far as you have to go to find me, even if that's all the way to Oregon."

"No, no, no," Marie said. "You cannot make me go without you."

"There is no choice," Zeke said. "If there was another way, we would do it."

Though it took a moment, Marie at last set her jaw and nodded her head, screwing her resolve to the wagon.

"I'll do what I have to do," she said.

Zeke put an arm behind her head and pulled her close, holding her for what he knew might be one last time. But he was careful not to stay too long.

"I'm going to take just what I need to get me to the next fort," Zeke said. "Nothing more."

That wasn't entirely true. For a three hundred mile journey, under other circumstances, Zeke would have taken food enough to last him five or six days. Now, he took what he reckoned to be the bare minimum to get him through two days. He could go a day or two without food if it became necessary. What he did take was powder and shot for his rifle – a substantial portion. Many a traveler on the Oregon Trail set out with an unrealistic expectation of the danger posed by Indians. Children in towns all over the eastern United States grew up on stories of savage attacks against settlers. What Zeke and his brother both knew was that, in truth, those pioneers crossing the overland route had more to fear from disease and accident than they did from Indians.

But that didn't mean the threat of Indian attack was nothing. And there were bandits, too. Especially near the Mississippi and Mid-Western settlements.

A solitary man with two horses presented an easy target, even for a small band of Indians. Zeke knew that he would face obstacles and dangers in the three hundred-mile journey to Bridger's Fort, obstacles and dangers enough that he might never make it to his destination. Nevertheless, he did not intend to become a victim of marauders.

When they decided to make the overland trip together, Elias Townes bought for himself and his brother matching percussion rifles manufactured by H.E. Leman. They were fine weapons, the both of them, and as accurate a rifle as Zeke had ever shot. Elias also bought them both a Colt Paterson – the Number 5 Holster gun. Since the day they'd crossed the Missouri, Zeke had carried the Paterson revolver in a holster strapped to his saddle. On those days when he spared the horse and walked beside the wagon, he left the saddle gun tucked behind the front board of the wagon where he could get at it quickly. He always kept his cap box on his belt, and the Leman rifle and his powder horn remained as easily accessible as the saddle gun.

With five shots in the Paterson and one in the rifle, Zeke knew he could put down six Indians or bandits before he ever had to reload. He'd grown up shooting with his father and brothers in the backwoods of Kentucky, and he didn't have any doubts about his marksmanship.

"I'm going to take Towser with me," Zeke said, speaking of one of the four dogs the family had with them.

"Do not feed him your food," Marie said.

"He can find his own food. Probably better than me. He'll be all right. He's good company, and he'll go farther and faster than any of the other dogs."

Zeke hesitated. Towser was a good dog.

"Unless you want to keep him here with you."

"No. Take him."

Zeke didn't share with his wife his true reason for taking one of the dogs. If it came to it, he would hate to have to do it. He wasn't lying when he said that Towser was a good dog.

A whisper went round the circled wagons.

"Elias Townes intends to kill Marcus Weiss!"

Several people had seen Elias come down from the hilltop where he'd gone to talk to his brother, and they misread the determined look on his face. They watched him return to his own wagon where he went into his stores and fetched rifle and powder and shot. No one bothered to ask him what he intended to do with these things, they just reached their own conclusions and began spreading their gossip.

Not that Elias Townes cared a whit what they said.

When he turned with rifle in one hand and revolver in the other to walk to the wagons at the back, it only confirmed the gossips in their opinions. Others, hearing the whispered rumor, denied it. Elias wouldn't, they said. But none could deny as his long strides carried him away from the circled wagons to the others hanging off at the back, that Elias Townes was unnecessarily armed and walked with a purpose.

Marcus Weiss certainly took a second look as he saw Elias coming toward him, rifle in hand, and the German emigrant kept his eyes on the wagon train's elected leader.

But Elias passed by Weiss's wagon and walked to his brother's wagon at the back of the line.

Ezekiel was just finishing saddling his horse, a dark chocolate bay. He'd already packed a pannier on a dappled gray with a black mane. The gray was his favorite saddle horse, named to remind him of home whenever he traveled. He called the horse Duke. Typically, he'd have put the pannier on the bay, but he wanted to give Duke a bit of a rest today.

Marie stood nearby, the young Daniel at her hip. She watched her husband with wet eyes. Elias nodded his head in greeting but found himself unable to speak to her. His guilt at sending away his brother – Marie's husband and Daniel's father – overwhelmed him.

"I want you to take these," Elias said, holding out the rifle and reaching for the saddle gun.

"I ain't taking your guns, Elias," Zeke said.

"I brought half a dozen rifles with me," Elias said. "I won't be lacking for armaments, neither for hunting nor protection. But you should have these guns to protect yourself. A single rifle and a holster gun won't be enough if you run into trouble."

Zeke shook his head again and held up a hand, but Elias insisted.

"You take these. It could make the difference whether you reach Bridger's Fort or not."

Zeke frowned and shook his head.

"If you need these guns, I'll be sorry to have them," Zeke said.

"If I need these guns, I have others," Elias countered. "If you need these guns –" but then he stopped what he was saying with a glance at Marie. "Well, if you need these guns, you'd better have them with you. It'll ease my conscience a mite if you'll take them."

"All right," Zeke relented, taking the rifle and leaning it against his wagon and tucking the holstered Paterson into his belt.

"And this," Elias said. "Take this, also."

He held out a small burlap sack now with a bit of twine cinching the top closed, and Zeke took it, feeling a surprising weight. He pulled the twine to release the top and looked inside. Dozens of coins were in the sack.

"It's one hundred dollars," Elias said. "Enough money to see you through the winter and buy your way into a wagon train next spring, should you have to do that."

"I won't take your money, Elias," Zeke said.

"It's your money, too. It's your portion of the money we're using to start our business in the Pacific Northwest. We can't start a business if you're not there, so it's an investment in our future plans."

Zeke frowned. He glanced at Marie and dropped his voice, turning slightly so that he was facing away from her.

"You know there's small chance that you'll ever see me again," Zeke muttered. "This is a lot of money for a corpse."

Elias shook his head.

"Then don't get yourself killed. I won't argue this with you, Zeke. You take the money and you make it to Fort Bridger. You can pay me back when we're reunited and getting started in our business."

Zeke swallowed. He didn't like it, but he wouldn't argue. If he did make it to Fort Bridger, Elias was right that he would need money to buy his way into a wagon train and to supply himself. If Marie and Daniel wintered with him at Fort Bridger, they would need almost all new supplies come spring. Even if he found a job and worked at the fort through the winter, whatever meager wages he earned wouldn't pay his way to Oregon City.

"Another option to consider," Elias said.

"Yes?"

"When we meet back at Fort Bridger, I might force a split in the wagon train. Those who want can travel with us – your family and mine and our hired men. I'm sure plenty would come along with us. The others can make their own way. If their wives won't travel with you, we will leave them to themselves."

Zeke grinned.

"I would prefer that over trying to get on with another train."

Elias nodded.

"Then we'll see about it at Fort Bridger. But if there is opportunity for you there to get on with another train, take it. My reluctance to split away from this company is that these people are trusting me with their lives, and I would not feel right abandoning them."

Zeke nodded.

"I'll make a decision, and if I go on ahead, I'll leave word."

Henry Blair saddled a horse quickly and rode out in pursuit of Zeke Townes.

Blair, a young man, younger by a couple of years than Zeke, had hired on with the Townes Party back in Independence. He was the closest thing they had to a wagon train captain, and only because he'd been west a couple of years back. He'd worked as a trapper and wintered at Bridger's Fort, but returned to Missouri in '45. He'd been a good hand, and he'd proved his worth along the journey so far. When they'd camped at Chimney Rock, it was Blair who suggested an inventory. The pioneers needed to know at what rate they were going through their supplies so they would better be able to restock at Fort Kearney. At Fort Laramie, he'd recommended the party buy additional rope.

"You'll pay top dollar for it, but when it comes to the steep parts where you have to lower the wagons by hand, you'll be glad you've got it," Blair had said.

Other than being a willing hand, he wouldn't be able to help them much beyond Bridger's Fort. He'd trapped in the nearby mountains, but he hadn't exactly followed the trail. But he was a good hand, and Elias Townes had sought his opinion on any number of matters so far, and Blair didn't have to worry that he'd earned his keep.

Now he charged out from the camp, rising up over a hill and down into a hollow and then over another hill, and there he caught sight of his quarry.

"Mr. Zeke!" Blair shouted. "Mr. Zeke! Hold up one moment!"

Zeke had left camp at a lope, unwilling to linger longer than necessary.

Saying goodbye to his wife and son had been the hardest part. Now he wanted to get far enough away that he couldn't change his mind – go back for Marie and Daniel. He'd already started telling himself that the three of them, with their dogs and horses, their wagon and oxen, could make it as far as Bridger's Fort. He'd already started telling himself that where they wintered was less important as wintering together. He'd already started telling himself that he could keep his wife and son safe for three hundred miles.

He didn't believe these things, but he knew it wouldn't take much to convince himself. Parting from them had crushed his spirit. So he rode fast.

But he'd slowed the bay and Duke down to a walk now. He did not hear Henry calling over the wind, but Towser started to bark and Zeke looked back – though he'd told himself he wouldn't – and saw the rider approaching.

For the moment of half a heartbeat, Zeke had hope that maybe they'd changed their minds. Maybe the women saw the outcast riding away from his family and took pity on him, or on Marie, and the women who said they would not travel with him had changed their minds.

But he knew that wasn't going to be the case as he pulled up on the reins and waited as Henry Blair traversed the grassy ground at a gallop.

As Henry rode up even with Zeke, he dragged reins. He was breathing hard from the gallop.

"Mr. Zeke," Henry said, gasping for air.

"What is it, Henry?" Zeke said.

Henry held up a finger to give himself a moment to breathe. Then he reached into his vest and took out a piece of paper.

"I've made you a map to Bridger's," Henry said. "But it's important that you hear this. All the water out through here is alkali, Mr. Zeke. It's bad water. It'll kill the horses, for sure, and if you drink enough of it, it'll kill you, too."

Zeke glanced at the dog.

On purpose, he'd taken only a little water, wanting to leave plenty for Marie and Daniel.

Henry held out the paper and Zeke took it.

"Independence Rock," Zeke said, reading the paper. "The July Fourth landmark. We should beat the snow in the mountains if we're at Independence Rock by July Fourth."

"That's right," Henry said. "It's a wide mound, but not high like a mountain. Maybe it's a hundred feet high. But you'll know it, because all the travelers who've come the trail ahead of us have scratched or painted their names onto the rock."

"I have had it in my mind to do the same," Zeke said. "And what is Devil's Gate?"

"The next landmark," Henry said. "After you pass Independence Rock, not ten miles away, you'll see the Devil's Gate. It's a narrow cleft, with the Sweetwater River running through it. It's twice as high as Independence Rock. Maybe even more than that. You can water your horses in that river. It's good water. The first thing you have to do is make it to Sweetwater River. If you don't, you'll lose the horses."

Zeke nodded.

"How far to good water, do you reckon?"

"Seventy miles. Eighty miles."

"I can make that."

"Beyond Devil's Gate, you'll go about a hundred miles and then cross the Sweetwater River again. That's where you come to the South Pass. That's the way through the mountains," Henry said. "The old trappers said it was the most important point on all of the Oregon Trail. They said if wasn't for South Pass, no wagon train would ever get to the Pacific Northwest. They said Oregon City might as well be on the moon."

"Why is that?"

"If it weren't for the South Pass, you'd have to take your wagons over the mountains, and that would just be too much," Henry said.

"Everybody who ever crossed the Missouri and set out west would be a go-backer. But like as not, you won't even realize it when you get there."

Zeke narrowed his eyes.

"Why will I not realize it?"

"It's just a flat, open expanse. It's the highest point on the trail, but it don't even seem like you're up high at all, the slope is so gradual."

It didn't take much for Zeke to believe it. The trail had been hard enough already, but he knew the hardest part still lay ahead of them. They still had mountains and desert in front of them. The tedium of the Platte River Territory, where there was water and good grass for grazing, was enough to make some turn around.

"But the other thing about the South Pass, it's pretty flat, open countryside. When you're at the summit – if you even notice – you'll be standing on the Continental Divide. That's not just the divide for which way the water flows, but it's also the halfway point from Independence, Missouri, to Oregon City, or pretty near to halfway. The pass is about twenty or thirty miles wide, so you don't even realize that you're in a pass. You'll see the Wind River Mountain Range north of you, but when you're in the pass, you won't realize how impossible it would be to try to get through either north or south."

Zeke nodded. He had the paper with the rough map to Bridger's Fort sketched out, but he wanted to fix all of this in his mind.

"So after the Devil's Gate, I'm looking for the Continental Divide on the South Pass. What's next?"

"After the Pass, it's the Sublette Cutoff. If you're making for Bridger's, you've got to take the south trail and not the Sublette Cutoff. The Sublette trail takes you straight west and you'll miss Mr. Bridger's Fort altogether. The fork in the trail for the Sublette

43

Cutoff, that's another hundred miles or so beyond the Devil's Gate. Then another hundred miles to Bridger's Fort."

All the same information was on the paper, and Zeke consulted it now.

"I'm eighty miles to Devil's Gate and fresh water," he said. "A hundred miles to the Sublette Cutoff. A hundred miles to Bridger's Fort."

"That's it," Henry said.

"Is there a landmark for the Sublette Cutoff? Something I can watch for?"

Henry shook his head.

"Fraid not, Mr. Zeke. That's just a grassy plain out there, flat as a flapjack, as wide open as the sky. It's a hard ground where nothing much of anything grows other than sagebrush and bunch grass. You just look for where the tracks split and take the lower trail. That's the one that'll take you to Bridger's. And beyond the cutoff, out of the South Pass, you'll come to the Green River. You'll have to cross the Green River and then Black's Fork before you get to Bridger's Fort."

Zeke sighed heavily. He had every confidence in himself, but the odds seemed long of staying away from trouble, either natural or man-made, and not getting lost.

"Trappers do it all the time," Henry Blair said. "They'd go into the mountains alone with just a couple of pack mules. Be gone for three or four months at a time. Some of them ol' boys I knew, why they were dumb as dirt. If they can manage it, you can manage it."

"Thanks, Henry," Zeke said, motioning with the piece of paper. He folded it and put it inside his vest. "Say, do you happen to know the date?"

Henry gave a rueful smile.

"Today's the first day of July."

Zeke looked up sharply.

"Eighty miles to Independence Rock?"

"Thereabouts."

"This wagon train won't make it by July Fourth."

Henry shook his head.

"No, sir. Be mighty close, but we'll miss it by a day or two."

Zeke touched the brim of his hat and nodded his thanks to Henry Blair.

"See you at Bridger's Fort," Zeke said.

"All right, Mr. Zeke. Keep your powder dry!"

5

───── ◦ ─────

WHAT A THRILL IT had been when they first saw Chimney Rock out on the horizon. It took three days of travel to reach it from when they first saw the towering rock on the far horizon.

When it was at last only a mile or so ahead, the children rushed forward, such was their excitement. They'd heard about it from their parents, of course, and the truth was that their parents were just as excited. Hadn't Zeke himself galloped forward on Duke?

They'd been so many days on the prairie, following the course of the Platte River, and there had been so much of nothing to see but the vast emptiness for so long, that a tall rock pointing to the Heavens had been sufficient to arouse the greatest excitement in children and adults alike.

It was like that at all the landmarks and forts, children and adults thrilled at the prospect of seeing the next thing, not simply because it meant they were closer along on their journey, but the landmarks themselves were curiosities worthy of note.

But that first afternoon, leaving the wagon train behind, he'd felt no excitement at seeing Register Cliff.

Henry Blair had talked about it earlier in the trip, and the pamphlet map that Elias carried mentioned the sandstone cliff rising one hundred feet above the Platte. Blair and the pamphlet both said that travelers inscribed their names on the cliff – just as they did at Independence Rock and other landmarks along the way. But now Zeke found his enthusiasm had waned. He didn't even bother riding to the rock to see the names there, much less carve his own.

"I'll do it at Independence Rock," he said to himself.

Zeke had ridden several miles to get out in front of the wagon train that first afternoon, going on until dark.

He sweated through the afternoon, resisting the urge to drink from his canteen. He'd taken only a little water with him, preferring to leave as much as he could for Marie and Daniel. Somewhere up ahead, he didn't know how far, he would encounter the Sweetwater River, and from what Henry Blair said, that was where he could again drink and water the horses. Until then, he would have to keep Towser and the horses out of whatever water he encountered.

When dusk caught up to him, Zeke camped down at the base of a small rise, hoping that would be sufficient to block some of the wind.

His face was raw from the wind. His lips stung.

He unburdened the horses and picketed them in the best patches of grass he could find, and he then collected handfuls of sagebrush. He made up a small fire with the sage, just something to warm his hands over. He cut a piece of the cured bacon and gave it to Towser so that the dog would have some supper after walking all afternoon.

On the trail, with the wagons, Zeke periodically lifted one or the other of the family dogs into the back of the wagon so that they might get a brief rest. The wagons moved slow enough, though, that a full day of travel never taxed one of the dogs. Even at the end of the day, Towser always had energy enough for a game of fetch if a stick could be found.

But mounted on the bay and with Duke in tow, Zeke had traveled faster than the wagons by quite a bit, and at times Towser had struggled to keep up. When he fell too far behind, Zeke would drop down from the saddle and rest the horses, and when Towser caught up, Zeke would lift him up into the saddle and ride with Towser in his lap. Or, he would just walk and lead the horses, and then the dog had no trouble keeping up.

As night settled in, and the temperature dropped, Zeke rolled out a blanket to sleep on and then pulled a quilt over him for warmth. Towser laid down on the blanket beside Zeke, and the dog helped to keep him warm through the night.

"This is why I wanted to bring you along, pal," Zeke said, hugging the dog close to him. Towser didn't seem to mind. They would keep each other warm. "Maybe if we work together we can both survive this."

If it came to it that Towser didn't survive, Zeke knew he would feel terrible. He'd always had dogs, all his life, and there'd always been a favorite. He'd had a dog once when he was a not yet a teenager, aptly called Trouble. A yellow dog, good as gold, and full of muscle. Ol' Trouble would run all day and night, given the chance, but he was the sort of dog who'd stick his snout in a snake hole or scare cattle for fun. Trouble got trampled by a team of horses pulling a wagon, and it still bothered Zeke to this day to think of it. He'd witnessed the moment, and for the longest time, he couldn't even talk about that dog because he was so bothered by it. He'd been calling Trouble, but the dog just ignored him, barking like mad at the horses until he got too near and spooked one of them. They'd charged forward and run him down. That was a terrible day. The man driving that wagon had berated Zeke as he pulled his dying dog from under the wagon.

He'd always been soft when it came to animals. If it came down to it, he didn't know if he'd be able to choose his own survival over Towser's.

"Oh! These ferocious thoughts that steal sleep," Zeke said out loud.

The ferocious thoughts were not finished with him, either.

His own troubles worried him enough, but he could not escape worrying over the troubles of his wife and son.

There were men enough to see to their needs. Caleb Driscoll, the Tucker brothers and the Page brothers, and Jerry Bennett. They were all hired hands who worked for the lumber mill back in Kentucky and chose to make the journey to Oregon when Elias and Zeke announced that they were going west. They were all young men, and other than the Tuckers who were married, they had no family of their own to see to. They would watch out for Marie and Daniel. And of course Elias would, too. But Elias had his own family.

But what if they all fell to hardship? What if Zeke went on with another wagon train and the Townes Party encountered snow in the Blue Mountains? If they were snowed in, trying to survive the winter without enough food, Marie and Daniel would endure hardships that would be beyond Zeke's ability to help them. If they met snow in the winter, it would be every man, woman, and child for themselves.

And Zeke would be warm and fed in Oregon City. He couldn't bear the thought of it.

"Get out of there!" Zeke called. "Towser! No!"

The dog obeyed, but reluctantly.

Even Duke pulled at the creek with Zeke pulling against the reins. They were all thirsty. Zeke poured water from his canteen onto his hand to moisten the horses's lips and tongues. He poured just a little water into a bowl and let Towser lap it up. He just touched a few drops into his own mouth.

He'd dismounted, trying to ease the burden on Duke some. The bay carried the pannier, but there wasn't hardly enough in there to even try to lighten the bay's load. And the four of them – Zeke, the two horses, and the dog – hiked out across the countryside.

They followed the North Platte River, but not too close. Zeke worried if they were too near the river, the horses would go down to it to drink. Here, with the ribbon of cottonwoods lining the banks of the Platte in sight, Zeke could give a tug to the lead ropes and the horses would give off trying to get to the water. But if they were nearer, the horses might fight him, and there was nothing he could do to stop them then.

All through the late morning and early afternoon, Zeke carried the sun like a pack on his back – the heat of it like a constant, unrelenting weight pressing down on him.

He felt the sweat in his pants, down the back of his shirt, under his arms, inside the band of his hat. His socks felt like wet rags wrapped around his feet.

He wanted more than anything – needed more than anything – a good long drink of clear water. He could easily turn the bottom of his canteen toward the sky and just drink. But all the water in the world that he could drink right now was what he carried in his canteen, and that wasn't enough to get him to fresh water. He had to ignore the heat and his parched mouth and the yearning from his body for water.

His lips and face were raw from the sun and the wind and the salt from his own sweat. The wind was as relentless as the sun. Somehow, it offered no relief from the heat of the sun. It was a hot wind that blew.

If he could find a shady spot, a grove a trees, Zeke would rest through the afternoon and resume the trail come dark. But other than the cottonwoods down by the Platte, there wasn't a tree on the horizon. And there, he'd have to fight what would almost surely be a losing battle against the horses and the dog to keep them from drinking the poisoned water.

Zeke didn't know what made water alkali. He assumed it was minerals leaching out of the ground. All he knew for sure was that he would lose his horses and his dog if he let them drink from the water. He told himself that maybe a little wouldn't hurt them, but he didn't know at what point a little became too much. And once they started drinking, he didn't know how he would make them stop.

So, he kept going. One foot and then the next.

"We're not go-backers!" Zeke shouted against the wind.

It was mid-afternoon now, Zeke's third day alone on the trail, counting that first afternoon by himself. On Henry Blair's hand-sketched map, he estimated the distance to Independence Rock was one hundred and fifty miles. Zeke figured he'd done something close to eighty miles of that. Maybe ninety. Either way, he was better than halfway, so long as Blair's estimation was correct.

"My Lord, it's a trudge, though," Zeke said. "Come on, Towser! We'll get there."

An empty, horrible land, rolling hills of grass interrupted only by bare sandstone rocks and patches of sagebrush. The only relief – the cottonwoods and the North Platte the only relief in sight, and those as dangerous as seeking relief beside a rattlesnake.

At times, when he crested a high hill, Zeke could see a small mountain rising up over his left shoulder. He had a sense that he was following the river's course around the mountain, but so often he dipped down into hollows, and when he came out he found himself below larger rises that obscured his view. Following the river meant always being near the lowest spot on the landscape, but sometimes, at the tops of hills, he managed to get a peek at the countryside he was missing.

At some point, Zeke decided to cinch tight the saddle and ride again. He kept a close watch on Towser to make sure he wasn't wandering toward the water that would kill him.

Through the afternoon, Zeke kept going, though the pace was plenty slow. They all suffered from exhaustion and thirst. Zeke grew so thirsty that he stopped even thinking about the aching in his stomach for lack of food.

The day before, when they stopped to camp, Zeke had thrown the stick for Towser several times. The dog's energy seemed to never wane. Now, though, he thought he wouldn't have the strength even to toss a stick.

Toward dusk, the river – and the trail – began to make a long bend. The sun, in his face most of the afternoon, was now on Zeke's right shoulder. He'd turned to the south. Henry Blair's map was mostly straight lines from one landmark to the next, so consulting the map did not help. But Zeke prayed a silent prayer that the turn to the south meant they'd soon be encountering the Sweetwater River.

At last, staying up away from the river, Zeke drew reins and made to stop for the night.

He poured a little water into a tin bowl for Towser.

He poured a little water into his hand and used it to get Duke's lips wet. He gave the bay mare a little water in the same fashion. And he took the tiniest sip for himself. When he'd finished, Towser was looking expectantly at him.

"I wish there was more I could give you," Zeke said. "It seems cruel to give such a small bit and no more."

And with a sigh, he decided there was. He took another small sip himself. He poured a little more on his hand for the bay mare, a little more for Duke. A little more into the tin bowl.

Towser was careful with what he had, not splashing it all over the place.

Zeke returned the cork to the canteen. It took all his will not to have another drink.

6

— · —

ELIAS TOWNES CUT A dashing figure atop the palomino he called
Tuckee. All the women in the train thought so, and even the men
had to grudgingly acknowledge an admiration for Elias Townes.
Elias was tall and lean, and every movement spoke of strength.
Whether Elias was the best man to lead the wagon train was a subject
open to debate. There were older, more experienced men. Captain
Walker had been a viable candidate. But Elias looked the part, and
that had been enough to get him elected.

Like his brother, he'd named his horse to remind him of home.

"Whoa, Tuckee," Elias called. The horse stood atop a hill ahead
of the wagon train. The train was cutting its way through a narrow
hollow, a terrible place to make camp, but over this rise the ground
leveled out some and would make a good place to stop for the night.

The third day since he'd turned out his own brother, and Elias had
spent all of the previous two days riding ahead, looking for signs that
Zeke had passed this way. More than that, he was watching for signs
that Zeke had run into trouble. Maybe he'd find the horses or the
dog. Maybe he'd come across his brother's body. His fear was that if
he didn't ride ahead and find it first, Marie might see. The thought
of it twisted his stomach into knots.

Captain Walker was riding his black gelding, a horse he bought in Independence just before setting out. The horse wasn't nearly as saddle ready as the captain was made to believe back in Independence, but after almost a thousand miles, the gelding had become a pretty good horse under saddle.

"Looks like a good place to camp," Captain Walker said.

"My thoughts, too," Elias said.

"No sign of your brother?"

Elias shook his head.

"I wouldn't have thought there would be, though. He can make it to Bridger's Fort without any problem."

"Indians would be the only problem," Captain Walker said without any sympathy. "I know the Indians we fought in Florida were hellish savages, and I've heard the Plains Indians are no better. General Jesup found that the only way to deal with them was to starve them out. Destroy their homes, destroy their resources, and force them to submit."

"Huh," Elias said. He didn't care for talk of the government forcing anyone to submit to anything. Elias and Zeke and their brothers and sisters had all been raised by a frontiersman who had no use for government.

"I suppose it'll be the same here in the West," Captain Walker said. "I hope it don't come in my lifetime, though. It's hard to imagine how you would fight the Indian out here in this country where it goes on forever in every direction. We had a hard enough time fighting them on the peninsula where the oceans trapped them from three ways."

Elias made another noncommittal grunt.

"All the Indians we've encountered have been friendly enough," Elias said.

"That'll change," Walker said. "A few more years of hundreds of people crossing this trail, and the friendly attitude will give way. Or the first time someone discovers gold on a tribe's hunting grounds. The government will tell the Indians they have to leave, and the Indians will tell the government they won't. Then it'll be a fight. Can you imagine? Trying to fight the Indians in this territory? You're lulled half to sleep riding out across these hills and hollows, and then you top a hill like this one and down below you are a thousand warriors – you've walked into them and had no idea they were there. That's what I'd be worried about with your brother. He'll make fresh water, and he'll get to Bridger's Fort. But my fear would be that he'd top one of these hills and see a half dozen braves of the Plains and get hisself scalped."

"Thank you, Captain Walker," Elias said, not attempting to disguise the shortness in his tone. "Would you pass the word to circle the wagons when they get below this rise? I'd like to make camp here tonight."

Walker, who seemed oblivious that his thoughts on Zeke's well-being weren't wanted, nodded his head.

"Happily," he said. "I'm sure we could all use some supper."

Walker wheeled the black and started back down the hill to spread the word.

Elias rode Truckee out across the crest of the hill and down into another hollow farther beyond. The horse loped at a pretty good pace and brought him back up another rise. All he found was empty grassland. Finding nothing was better than finding something, but he hated not knowing how his brother fared.

He patted the horse on the neck.

"If anything happens to Zeke, I'll never forgive myself," Elias said.

7

JOHNNY HUBBARD RAMMED HOME the lead ball.

A woman screamed amid all the chaos, and she caught his attention. He glanced in the direction of the sound and saw the woman running. She stumbled and went down on all fours. It was Winthrop chasing her, and he caught her now. He had a club in his hand, raised up over his head. He brought it down, but the woman rolled onto her back, and Winthrop missed her entirely. He grabbed her by the deerskin blouse she wore and hefted her up in the air with one hand and then dropped her roughly back to the ground.

Johnny saw the blade in her hand. He saw the sweeping motion of it as it made its arc through the air. Winthrop let out a yelp and jumped back, letting go of her blouse. He wrapped his arm around his cut torso. Johnny could see that Winthrop was hurt, but he swung the club a second time, and this one connected with a thud against the side of the woman's head. She fell back, dazed. Winthrop swung the club a second time, and then he dropped down on her, his knees pinning her shoulders to the ground.

Johnny Hubbard figured that was more than needed to be done. Two good licks to the head with that club, and the woman probably wasn't getting up again. But it wasn't Johnny's gut that was cut open, and if Winthrop wanted to pin a dead woman's shoulders to the ground, that was his business.

He grabbed the woman by the hair and held her head up at an awkward angle. He dropped the club beside his knee and came out with his big knife. Two quick cuts at the hairline, and then he slid the knife right over the top of her skull.

Hubbard's fingers moved to the cap box on his belt. Nimbly, skillfully, he positioned the cap on the nipple under the rifle's hammer, and then he put the rifle into his shoulder. His eyes swept the hectic scene, seeking a target.

A boy, maybe eleven- or twelve-years-old, surged forward with a spear, charging toward Neil Rimmer. Neil had his knife hilt deep in a woman's abdomen, and his back was turned to the boy.

Hubbard squeezed the trigger, dropped the hammer on the rifle, and watched at the bullet smashed into the boy's chest, jerking him off his feet and stopping his run.

"That was a good shot," Hubbard said to himself with a grin.

A rifle cracked, and then another.

Hubbard quickly bit the cap from his powder horn and poured out a quantity into the gun. Most of the other men used paper cartridges, but Johnny Hubbard preferred to shoot the way he learned growing up – measuring his own powder – patch and ball. He was just as fast loading the rifle as any of the others using paper cartridges.

He bounced the ramrod once to be sure the ball was seated tight. Already his eyes were searching for a target, and he knew where he wanted to put this next shot. A woman had been hiding in the middle of the camp under some brush, but just as Hubbard started to load the rifle, the woman sprang up and started to flee the camp. She was a young woman, and the size of her belly suggested she was pregnant.

Hubbard squeezed the trigger again and put her down.

Some of the boys had their fun with the women and then cut their throats. Others preferred to just do the killing they came to do.

Maybe it had been five minutes since they launched the attack on the camp. Maybe it was closer to ten. Johnny Hubbard couldn't say for sure one way or another. But this was a good group of men. They knew their business and were fast about it. Already he could see some of them toting three or four scalps a piece.

There were seventeen of them in the outfit, and he figured the camp held something close to forty women and children, plus a few old men. Outside of Winthrop getting cut across the belly, it didn't look like any of the boys had any injuries worse than some fingernail scratches.

The chaos was dying down. One woman was screaming. She'd been shot through the back and was on the ground. A few others, women and children, were moaning or sobbing, but it was just the one screaming. Neil Rimmer had a woman on the ground, his pants down around his ankles and her dress jerked up, and she was shouting muffled curses. He had his hand clamped over her mouth, but she was wriggling and putting up a fight.

"Kill anyone that ain't dead yet!" Hubbard shouted. "Let's finish this and get out."

Their husbands would be gone for at least a couple of weeks, maybe even a couple of months. Trouble was, Johnny Hubbard didn't know how long they'd already been gone, and it sent a chill through him to think of what they'd do if the men from this camp turned up now. Likely, they wouldn't be back here for days or even weeks, and by then Hubbard and his outfit would be well on their way to Missouri. Still, he didn't want to stay around here any longer than they had to.

"Finish up there, Neil!" Johnny Hubbard shouted.

Neil Rimmer let out a howling laugh.

"Talk to her! Don't talk to me! She's the one causing the trouble."

8

Zeke stood still as a statue beside the cottonwood tree, his hat in one hand and the thin linen cord wrapped around the wooden spool in the other.

"Come on, now," Zeke whispered, his eyes on the cicada as it landed on a branch. "Don't you move."

He took a half step forward, and the bug started to chirp. Amazing how loud they could be. There must have been a hundred of them down along the banks of the North Platte, chirping and buzzing their wings.

Zeke struck as fast as he could, sweeping his arm up in a big arc so that he brought his hat down onto the cicada. In one motion, he caught the bug and dropped to his knees, trapping the bug against the ground and under his hat.

"Gotcha!" Zeke declared.

He set the spool aside and then lifted the hat, giving it a good shake to stun the bug, and then flipping it over. Before the cicada could fly away, Zeke grabbed it in his hand. Now he sat down, holding the bug tight even as its wings tickled against his palm and fingers. He fed some of the cord off the spool and made a loop out of it. He had to use his teeth to tie the cord off. Then he put the loop around the cicada and slid it tight. He'd stuck an iron hook into the fabric of his vest, and he now twisted it out and tied it to the cord.

"All right, let's see who thinks you look tasty," Zeke said.

He'd already made a rod, cutting a branch from a willow he'd found growing among the cottonwoods on the bank of the North Plate, and he'd attached a stronger hemp cord to the willow rod. Now he tied the hemp and linen cords together, and in the last bit of dusk cast his line out to the surface of the river. He couldn't drink the water, but he could eat the fish.

Over his shoulder, Zeke heard Towser let out a yelp. The dog wasn't happy about being tied with the horses, but Zeke didn't want Towser following him down to the river.

The cicada flapped and buzzed on the surface of the water, but no fish jumped.

Zeke pulled the line in and gave it another toss. He walked a short ways along the bank and tried the line again in what looked to be a deeper hole. The cicada jerked on the surface of the water, and a trout as big as Zeke's thigh jumped and caught the bug and the hook. Zeke gave a tug and a twist to the line to set the hook.

Towser gave a screeching bark.

"Hang on, partner!" Zeke called to the dog, walking back and pulling up on his makeshift rod. "Supper's coming!"

Fresh trout from the North Plate.

Zeke cleaned the fish there by the riverbank. He collected cottonwood branches from the ground, and he took all of it back up to where he'd made his camp.

He'd picketed both horses in good grass and they seemed content enough. If the thirst got to them too bad, they'd run in the morning. If he lost them, he'd have a tough time making it to the Sweetwater.

As he made up his fire using sagebrush to get it started, Zeke reminded himself how important it was that he be deliberate in everything he do, especially as thirst, hunger, and exhaustion started to cloud his mind. He'd have to manage the horses. If they got bad thirsty, one or both might be liable to make a run for the river. But if that happened, there'd be little he could do to stop them. Best he could do was make sure he wasn't standing in the way and get trampled.

He cooked the fish, putting it skin-down directly on the coals. The cottonwood wasn't the best for cooking. The wood never did burn very hot. But he he had an endless supply of sagebrush he could push into the fire to add fuel, and he used his knife blade to push hot coal in under the fish until it had a nice pink hue.

He put a large portion of the fish into the bowl he'd been using for Towser, and then Zeke ate the rest of it himself. He'd never been much of a praying man. Marie prompted whatever prayers were said over their suppers, but tonight, as the sun dropped below the horizon and the vast array of stars began dotting the sky above, Zeke found himself praying a prayer of thanks.

"This ain't the circumstances I wanted, and it seems a sight more difficult than even what I'd counted on, but I'm grateful God that you saw fit to put cicadas on the river banks and trout big enough to eat them in the river. Thank you for the meal."

It felt like a weak prayer, but Zeke also felt a little better for saying it. The Lord had put the South Pass cutting through the mountains and He'd put green valleys full of fertile soil in Oregon Territory; He'd put bugs big enough to catch and tie a linen cord to down in the cottonwoods, and He'd put fish worth catching in water that couldn't be drunk. Now it was just up to Zeke to figure out what else the Lord had put in his path that might help him get to Oregon.

9

"WE NEED TO MAKE tracks out of the Winds fast as possible," Neil Rimmer muttered.

"We're making 'em," Johnny Hubbard said, and he clicked his tongue at his horse.

"We ought to move faster. If the men from that camp turn up, even in another day or two, they'll find us. And then it'll be our hair decorating some lodgepole."

"Maybe you ought not to have defiled that woman," Hubbard said. He never could understand a man who could have his way with a woman he was about to kill. He'd known men like Rimmer before – white men and Indians alike – but it confounded him. To Hubbard, it was one thing to kill an Indian woman and take her hair. He didn't hardly see any difference from shooting a deer or catching a fish. Hubbard had seen at an early age some of the worst atrocities committed by warring tribes, and he was convinced that Indians were more like animals than men. But he wouldn't have his way with an antelope before shooting it for supper.

"You got a weak stomach, Johnny?" Rimmer teased.

"I've got more scalps drying than you," Hubbard jabbed back. "All I'm saying is if you'd been a little quicker with the knife on your belt instead of the knife in your pants, maybe we could have left out of there a little faster."

Their group was winding down a trail leading out of the Wind River Mountains. They'd probably made ten miles from the camp already. But there was no getting around camping one night in the mountains. They'd need to camp by a stream somewhere, and take on as much water as possible before they dropped down into the South Pass.

Winthrop led the way out, having the most experience trapping in these mountains. Hubbard followed him, and Rimmer was just behind. The others trailed Rimmer. All of the men led a pack horse.

"What's your idea about a wagon train?" Winthrop asked.

Hubbard chewed his lip for a moment. This group had made three journeys to Bridger's fort and back over the last three years, bringing out supplies and returning with furs. Hubbard's thought was to build a fur trading company that would compete with biggest fur companies in the country, but so far they'd had little luck doing that. They had to rely on the trappers who were still working these mountains, and most of them were already trapping for one company or another.

That first year, going back with their wagons loaded with pelts, they'd been attacked by a band of Indians trying to steal their cattle. The Indians were few in number, and the attack didn't go well for them. They'd come on with knives and spears and been met by men who knew how to use a musket. When it was done, there were eight dead or dying Indian warriors on the ground, and they'd scalped them as a warning to any other parties that might want to try to steal their livestock.

But when they returned to St. Louis, they found the market for the Indian scalps was far better than that for the pelts. So the next year, they deliberately went looking for scalps.

Then this year, Bridger offered to buy all four of the wagons they'd brought out. He was willing to exchange pack horses for their teams. It meant no furs, and it meant no shelter in a storm. But the price Bridger offered for the wagons was too much to turn down.

Hubbard had the idea that if they were traveling light anyway, maybe they'd run into a small wagon train. And if they did, and they could work it, they should steal a couple of the wagons.

From the Missouri River to the Blue Mountains, the Emigrants Trail was full of abandoned wagons. Most of the folks who left their wagons did so beyond Bridger's Fort, but there were always a few between Fort Laramie and Bridger's Fort and sometimes even a couple along the Platte River – teams scattered or gave out, axles broke, wagons bogged down in mud, and the pilgrims found it was easier to walk it than to fight the oxen. When they abandoned the wagons, the emigrants buried their valuables. But it was always easy enough to find where the good stuff was buried.

So Hubbard concocted a plan. They wouldn't worry about furs, and they would sell their wagons to Bridger. They'd find a camp and take as many Indian scalps as they could. Then they would look for a wagon and a team that they could take back to the Missouri, and they'd fill it as they went.

"My idea is that if we can find a small wagon train, we ought to convince them to give us a wagon or two. On the trip back along the Platte, we'll just pick up any abandoned valuables we find along the way that's worth taking."

"Who's going to give us a wagon?" Rimmer asked.

Hubbard shook his head.

"People are generous wherever you go," Hubbard grinned. "Especially if they's shot in the skull."

Rimmer nodded his head.

"I reckon I can't argue with that logic."

10

Zeke poured a little water into his hand and let the bay take it from his hand. Duke seemed okay, but the bay's gums had started to lose some of the pink color. Zeke pressed a finger against the horse's top gum, and it took too long for the pale to start to disappear. The bay hadn't yet started to show signs of lethargy, but Zeke was worried.

Everything was dry grass now. The tracks of the wagon trains that had come on before had left the North Platte and its poisoned water, probably to keep livestock from running ahead to drink. But Zeke couldn't even see the tops of cottonwood trees down on the banks any longer. Mountains broke the horizon ahead, but Zeke couldn't say if they were twenty miles or a hundred miles away. He didn't know what mountains they were or if he'd keep on heading toward them or deviate somewhere. He thought he was facing straight west, but the sun was overhead, so he didn't even know for sure.

He also thought maybe he'd seen some rock formations before the mountains, but he wasn't sure about that. And now he'd dropped down below a rise in front of him, and he couldn't see what he'd thought were rock formations at all. "Not much longer," Zeke said. "We'll be to water soon."

He gave the bay a pat on the shoulder and then made a careless mistake. He blamed it on the lack of food, the lack of water, and the lack of sleep.

Zeke dropped the lead bay's lead rope, and the horse bolted. Duke gave a little dance, and looked to run, and Zeke lunged forward but too late. Duke took off behind the bay. And then Towser started to go, but Zeke shouted, "Hey! Towser! Come back here!"

The dog ran fifteen or twenty yards ahead, but when Zeke shouted his name again, Towser stopped and turned and looked back at him.

The two horses mounted the hill and then disappeared over the crest.

He might have wept, but instead Zeke uttered a furious string of oaths, and he kicked the dirt at his feet.

"Damnation!" he shouted. "My own foolishness."

Zeke shook his head and plucked his hat and wiped his face on his sleeve.

"Bless it all," he breathed.

Towser stood watching him, occasionally looking back in the direction the horses had gone.

"Damned horses," Zeke said, with a shake of his head. But the realization of the true horror was only now beginning to strike him. His guns. His powder and shot. His food – what little he had. He'd given the horses almost all the flour he brought, and he'd shared a lot of the bacon with Towser. But still, he'd now lost even the meager supplies. His fishing line and hooks were in the pannier. He couldn't even rig up a fishing pole.

The one saving grace was that he'd been giving the bay a little water, canteen in hand, and so he still had his canteen. Though there wasn't hardly water enough to drink in it.

He looked back over his shoulder. It wasn't an option to return to the wagon train. Banishment meant banishment. Banishment meant they wouldn't help him. Besides, he'd surely outdistanced them enough that with no water and no food, he'd never make it back to the train alive. Not on foot.

The only option available was forward. Somewhere there was fresh water. Sweetwater River. Independence Rock. The Devil's Gate.

"Well, we ain't gettin' closer by standing here," Zeke said. "Let's go, Towser."

The dog wagged his tail and watched Zeke approach. He stood still, waiting for a scratch on the head. Zeke realized he'd fed and watered the dog better than he'd fed and watered himself these last few days.

"It's going to be hard going for both of us from here on out," Zeke said, and he bent down and gave the dog a solid pat on the shoulder. "If you ever had it in your mind to make yourself useful and catch a rabbit, now would be a good time to do it."

And then Zeke realized he'd have to eat it raw. His fire starting kit – flint and char tin – was on Duke's back in the saddlebags.

11

——— • ———

WHEN IT CAME TIME to drop the cottonwoods, Elias Townes lifted an ax and threw his shoulders and back into the work as much as any man.

"We'll swim the cattle and float the wagons," Elias said. It was his constant refrain at every crossing.

They'd not lost a person in a river crossing, though they'd lost a fair few head of cattle, and Elias was determined to make it to Oregon City without a drowning on his conscience. They'd lost plenty of people on this trip to one thing or another, but if all it cost them was a day or two of labor to cut trees and build rafts, he'd sooner do that than risk a life.

When he was a young man, Elias and some of his friends built a barge, loaded it with local goods, and floated it down the Ohio to the Mississippi and on down to Memphis. There they sold the goods and the barge and then walked home to Paducah. The money they made from that trip allowed Elias to start his timber business. His summer on a barge, and just the fact that he grew up on the Ohio and Tennessee rivers, meant that Elias as much as anyone in the Townes Party was comfortable with the water. Some folks who never experienced deep, flowing rivers possessed a healthy fear of them, which was just as well.

Among the party were the Page brothers and Jerry Bennett, all men who worked for Elias, as well as a few men who were packing to Oregon, and they could all swim a horse across a river. All of them rode in the cow column at one time or another. Most of them didn't herd cattle for a living, but they'd become good hands over the last thousand miles.

They could work one raft faster than they could work two with everyone pitching in, and in a day they could move all thirty-two wagons across a river. They needed to drop four decent sized cottonwoods and split them in half. Then they would dig them out, making eight long canoes. From a fifth tree, they would cut four long boards that they could use to secure the eight canoes together. So far, most of the crossings they'd encountered had a good launch worked into the bank where they could drive the wagons right down to the water and roll them up onto the canoes. With some heavy barn pulleys, they could run two lines from one bank to the other. Most of the men put their backs into the work, and the wagons could be got across the river on these fast-made canoe barges.

"We sure could use Mr. Zeke today," Henry Blair noted as he worked an ax to knock off the limbs of one of the cottonwoods. He made the comment with a purpose, and said it in the direction of Marcus Weiss, who stood now leaning against his ax and wiping the sweat from his brow. Weiss shot him a look but made no comment in return.

The last few days had been increasingly unpleasant for Marcus Weiss and even some of the women in the train. The men, especially the young, single men who worked the hardest to keep the wagons moving, had become resentful in just a few short days that Zeke Townes had been banished. Zeke was worth two of most of the rest of them, and in the case of some of the older men – Captain Walker,

Reverend Marsh, and Marcus Weiss, especially – Zeke was worth three of them.

They'd arrived at the river crossing late in the previous afternoon and made their camp there that night. Gabriel Townes and some of the other teenage boys drove the cattle, oxen, and horses some distance to forage. The grass here was sparse where the livestock from other wagon trains in advance had grazed it thoroughly.

But now, Gabe came riding hard over a hill, his horse at a gallop.

"Pa!" Gabe shouted, and Elias held the swing of his ax, immediately recognizing his son's voice.

Elias saw Gabe coming at a gallop and dropped the ax and ran a short distance to meet him. The other men working on building the canoes also stopped, and most of them took at least a few steps toward the boy.

"Indians!" Gabe shouted. "They cut out a bunch of our steers!"

"How many of the cattle?" Elias asked.

"At least half," Gabe said, his voice shaking as his horse danced a circle. "The others are driving the herd back now."

"Tarnation," Elias muttered, angry with himself. They'd put boys in charge of seeing to the livestock, and boys might be able to watch the cattle, even round them up and bring them on back, but they couldn't protect the cattle from thieves.

"Our livestock is what feeds us to the Oregon Territory," Elias shouted to the men watching. "We starve before we get there if we don't bring them back."

"You're a fool!" Marcus Weiss said. "We'll all lose our scalps, every one of us. Leave the cattle and be glad the Indians didn't take the women."

Elias ignored him.

"I need a dozen volunteers to ride with me," Elias said. "Whoever doesn't come finishes out these canoes, but you do it with a rifle beside you in case the Indians attack here."

Captain Walker scrambled up the bank away from the trees, and then he broke into a half run, making for his saddle and horse up near his wagon. A few others went, too, and Elias did not wait to count them.

"Ride us back to where they took the cattle," Elias said. "When we get there, you get back here and help defend what remains of the herd."

"Yes, sir," Gabe said. A thousand miles on the trail had taught him not to challenge his father, no matter how desperately he wanted to ride along.

Henry Blair caught his horse and led him quickly toward Elias's wagons where his saddle waited.

"What's your plan, Mr. Townes?" Blair asked.

Elias already had the saddle on the back of the palomino Tuckee.

"I'd reckon those Indians are probably about half starved if they're willing to risk stealing guarded cattle," Elias said. "They'll be easy enough to catch because the cattle won't move fast. I'm hoping if we fire a few shots at them, there's a good chance they'll give up the cattle."

"There!" Gabe pointed. "We were grazing them there, and the Indians came down over that hill yonder."

It was no different than any other hill they'd encountered over the last few days. They'd been one hill and then another, one hollow and then another, ever since leaving Fort Laramie, but Elias had confidence that Gabe was able to distinguish which hill the raiding party came from.

"They rode down and cut out about half of the herd," Gabe said. "They was quick about it, too, but we didn't have a single rifle. There was nothing we could do expect to start driving what cattle we could back to the wagons."

Indeed, on the way out, they'd past the other teen boys driving the cattle back.

"I don't know if they saw that we was unarmed or if they saw that we was all young," Gabe said. "It was a brazen attack! They turned the cattle and went right back over that same hill."

"Go on back now," Elias said. "Stay with your mama and tell her not to worry. You did right by saving what cattle you could."

As Gabe rode off, Elias turned to his company of volunteer soldiers. He had all his hired men among them – Caleb Driscoll, the Tuckers, the Pages, and Jeremiah Bennett. Henry Blair was there, of course, and Captain Walker. Jefferson Pilcher and Noah Bloom both rode along as well, Noah Bloom's wife pregnant back at the wagons. Three of the packers who'd joined the wagon train were also there, knowing that if they lost cattle, they'd be the first among the group to go without fresh meat.

All of the men carried rifles, and some of them were adept with the firearms.

Elias cast a lingering look at Noah Bloom. Noah was a young man, though he already had three children. Three small children and a pregnant wife. He was a fool for trying this journey, but he'd sold off everything he owned to buy the wagon and get the stake for the land in Oregon Territory. What would his wife and those children do if Noah left his life out here on the plains and his scalp on some thieving Indian's lodgepole?

"Listen to me," Elias said, holding the reins tight against Tuckee's mane as the horse pranced in place. His dander was up, sensing Elias's own excitement. "We'll not engage these Indians in a real fight. We'll advance after them, fire a few shots if it's warranted, and we'll round up the cattle. If we can't get them all, we'll take whatever strays we can get. I'm not here to trade the lives of men for cattle – neither ours nor the Indians' if we can help it."

Captain Walker looked angry at the announcement, always eager for a fight, but he was a man who knew how to follow orders, and he didn't question Elias's command of the wagon train.

Elias turned Tuckee and drove hard now toward the hill that his son had pointed to, and the small company of men gave pursuit.

They galloped down through a little valley between two large hills and topped another hill. The boys had taken the cattle a couple of miles or so from the wagons, and just as Elias was beginning to wonder how far the Indians might have gotten, he saw a lone pine tree rising above a drop up ahead. He urged Tuckee forward and then drew reins when he reached the drop. He looked down over steep escarpments and into a long and wide valley, maybe two or three miles long before it again reached the rolling hills in the distance. And there, seven or eight Indians were trying to hurry along cattle that were in no hurry to get anywhere after walking all the way from Missouri.

The Indians and cattle were spread out over the valley, the nearest Indians less than two hundred yards from where Elias sat on Tuckee's back.

Quickly, Elias searched for a path down into the valley, and he found it to his left. Loading a rifle on horseback was no easy task, but Elias did it now, even as the other men rode up and joined him.

"We should kill them all," Captain Walker said. "It's just a handful, and it sends a message on behalf of the wagon trains that come after us."

"You're damned right it does," Elias said. "It sends the message that they should come with more warriors next time, and kill the men guarding the cattle. We'll shoot to scare them off until that fails."

Elias ripped the paper cartridge with his teeth and poured in the gunpowder. He rammed home ball and wad with the ramrod. Then he held the rifle out with one hand and pulled reins with the other, directing Tuckee down to the easy grade.

The Indians had seen them now, and as Elias rode down through the escarpments and came out into the valley, the Indians were giving war whoops and shouting.

Captain Walker was surely right. They could kill these Indians, and probably do so without a loss of life. But Elias didn't want that. He just wanted his cattle back.

One of the Indians, the one nearest to the oncoming emigrants, wheeled his horse, hatchet in hand, and charged.

Captain Walker drew reins. Like Elias, he'd already loaded his rifle, and he also carried a holster gun strapped to his saddle. He shouldered the rifle, now, and drew back the hammer. Walker squeezed the trigger and sent the lead ball flying. It caught the Indian in the chest and threw him off his horse.

"Charge!" Walker shouted, drawing his holster gun.

12

⸺ ◆ ⸺

WHEN ZEKE REACHED THE crest of the hill behind which he'd lost sight of his horses, he had a clearer view of the rock formations that he'd thought he'd seen from a much greater distance. They were not very far off, after all. The peaks he could see were still at least twenty miles, but the rock formations were not even half that distance.

But it was something in among the rock formations that caught his eye, and in that moment, Zeke felt a tremendous relief.

Almost directly ahead, but still several miles off, he saw daylight in the middle of one of the formations. He knew instinctively what it must be, the same as he'd known right away what Chimney Rock was when he first saw just the tip of it on the horizon.

"That's it, Towser," Zeke said, and the dog turned his head to Zeke because even a dog can sense the relief of a thirsty man who knows there's good water ahead. "That gap in the rocks, it was carved by the Sweetwater River. That's the Devil's Gate. It must be."

In spite of the heat, Zeke Townes felt a chill go up his spine and down his arms as he stood for several moments watching the daylight through the gap in the rocks.

He knew, though, that he should reach Independence Rock before he came to Devil's Gate, and he started now to look around. Ahead, much nearer, was a rounded rock protruding from the earth, not nearly as tall as the other rock formations ahead, but quite long. Someone had told him that Independence Rock looked like a whale on its side, and he could see how someone might think this one did. Damn if the horses hadn't also run off with his chisel. He'd have to forgo chiseling his name into the rock.

But that was a small nuisance. If he was near enough to Sweetwater River to see where it had cut through a rock formation, he'd be able to chisel his name on every damned rock he encountered in Oregon City. All the same, the tracks of the wagons that had come on before led to Independence Rock, and Zeke and Towser now made their way there.

He had no doubt about where he was, but his approach toward the whale-shaped rock only confirmed it. The grass all around was cropped down to nothing. If Elias and the Townes Party intended to camp here, they'd be taking their livestock well away from the trail to forage. And as he neared the rock, he could see on the side the white flash marks in the stone where people had chipped away at it to leave their marks.

It had been July the first when Zeke left the wagon train. That made today the fifth of July. He'd missed Independence Rock by one day. The wagon train, at the soonest, would be another three days arriving here, and probably closer to a week.

Still, before he reached Bridger's Fort they might easily overtake him, now that he was on foot.

Zeke took a breath when he reached the base of the big rock mound. He put his hand on the rock, wondering how many other travelers had reached this point with the same ache for water he now felt. He could almost feel the energy buzzing from the rock of all the travelers who'd come before him, all their hopes and fears laid at the base of this monolith.

"Come on, Towser," Zeke said to the dog. "I'll race you to the top."

The slope on the rock was such that Zeke could scale it with ease, though he had no intention of racing the dog. Towser ran on ahead when Zeke started up the side. Here and there as he scaled the dome rock he saw names scratched into the stone, though not as many as there were down near the base. His thinking in climbing to the top was to get a look at the terrain and see if he could find the Sweetwater River, and the fastest route to the fresh water. He intended to drink until he was fully engorged, and then he intended to drink some more.

Though the new angle prevented him from seeing sky through the Devil's Gate notch in the rock formation, he could still see the notch itself, and once he reached the top of Independence Rock, Zeke thought he would trace the path of the river from there. But then Towser started barking angrily when the dog reached the top of the rock, and Zeke hoped it was neither snake nor body that had the dog so disrupted.

He took long strides as he neared the top, and the view gave Zeke a feeling that must have been very much like the one Moses had when he saw Canaan. For there, not two hundred yards to the south, he could see the winding and turning path of the Sweetwater River. Unlike the North Platte, the Sweetwater had no line of cottonwoods following its banks. Even from just a couple of hundred yards away, the river was imperceptible until Zeke climbed high enough up the rock to get a bird's eye view.

And even better, both horses were standing on the river bank.

"I'll be damned," Zeke said to Towser. "Maybe we're saved, after all."

Duke still had saddle and saddlebags on his back, but the bay had scatted a fair amount of Zeke's gear from the pannier. Zeke had everything strapped down and fitted in nice and snug so long as the horse never did more than a lope, but a gallop for water rattled everything loose. If he could find the chisel, Zeke intended to drink some water and then return to the top of Independence Rock once he'd recovered the horses and his gear.

He moved upstream of the horses and cupped his hands, dipping them down into the Sweetwater River. Zeke picked his face up from his hands and took a deep breath, the cool water dripping off his chin.

"That may be the best drink of water I've ever had," he said.

Zeke Townes made his camp there by the Sweetwater River and Independence Rock.

He found his chisel, and just before dusk he made a climb back up to the top of the rock. He held one of the saddle guns by the barrel and used the grip as a hammer, and he etched his name into the rock: "Ezekiel Townes July, 1846."

He watched the sun dip below the rock formations to the west. He wished he could see it slip into the crevice of the Devil's Gate – what a sight that would be. But he didn't have the right angle and didn't know how far he would have to go to get the angle. Maybe it wasn't even possible. But when the sun dipped below the western rocks, Zeke walked down off of Independence Rock.

At some point along the Platte, maybe it was in the shadow of Scotts Bluff, Zeke had the idea that he was probably as far east as he'd ever be again. Each step west brought him to a new "farthest point east." He did not foresee a time in his life when he would return. Not to Independence Rock, not to Fort Laramie, nor to Scott's Bluff. He certainly would not travel back to Kentucky where he'd left friends and family.

There had been little to enjoy about this journey. The tedium of the Platte River valley was broken only by the hardships, and there were worse hardships to come as the trail stretched westward. And now banishment over an act of self-defense. It was a cruelty to be abandoned by his own brother, and Zeke found himself now, in his loneliness, harboring hard feelings against his brother.

Elias Townes might have said a word and put all of this to an end. There might have been divided opinions, but none would have spoken against it.

Elias could have stood up on a cracker box and shouted for all to hear that Zeke's act was justified and any who didn't like it could find their own way. Not even Marcus Weiss would have gone against it. He might have complained. He might have started a whisper campaign against Elias and Zeke, but he wouldn't have left the wagon train, and none of the others would have left on his account.

It was bitterness seeping into Zeke's mind, picking away at his resolve.

"Come on," Zeke said, thinking about the sack of flour at the bottom of the Sweetwater River. "You're feeling sorry for yourself, and no amount of wallowing gets you closer to Bridger's Fort."

His water situation was resolved. He could follow the Sweetwater River much of the way through the South Pass. And beyond the South Pass, there'd be ample water – the Big Sandy and then the Green River – and then he'd be at the fort.

But Zeke was making up his mind about something else. At Bridger's Fort, he would insist to his brother that they abandon the wagon train. Let any who would come with them, but Elias wasn't going to make the rest of this journey without his family.

13

"CHARGE!" CAPTAIN WALKER YELLED, perhaps forgetting for the moment that he did not lead a company of infantry through the swampy heat of Florida, but instead was part of a small party of emigrants on the trail bound for the Pacific Northwest.

He drew his holster gun and pointed it toward the sky, thumbing back the hammer to release the trigger.

Elias Townes pulled reins to bring Tuckee to a stop again, and as the horse danced a circle, Elias tried desperately to get an aim with his rifle. He didn't want to fight these men. For all he knew, there were fifty warriors on the other side of this valley, rallying now to the sound of a rifle shot.

"Hold your fire!" Elias shouted, and he waved his rifle over his head, trying to stop the others. But their dander was up, and if anyone saw him, they took the waving rifle as encouragement.

Johnny Tucker drove hard out over the valley, making a sweeping arc around the cattle and up toward the Indians who were leading the herd. His brother Billy followed him close behind. As he neared the Indians, Johnny reined up and dropped from his saddle, rifle in hand. He ran a dozen yards out ahead of his horse and raised up the rifle.

Johnny was a deer hunter. His daddy had kept his family fed with his own musket, and Johnny was in the woods with his daddy, hunting even before he was big enough to lift a rifle. He squeezed his trigger, and even before the wind whipped away the puff of gray smoke, the others saw one of the Indians drop from the back of his horse.

Billy Tucker raced farther forward atop his horse while Johnny reloaded his rifle. Billy was every bit the hunter that Johnny was, but maybe because Billy was the younger of the Tucker brothers, he was prone to throwing fists. He'd never even pulled his rifle from its scabbard. Instead, he rode down one of the Indians. At a full gallop, Billy leaped across his horse, clutching the Indians around the throat and dragging the man from his horse and onto the ground.

They hit the earth with a heavy thud and Billy scrambled through the dirt until he was on top of the Indian. And then he commenced to flinging fists at the cattle thief, but in a moment he gave up. Billy stood up and backed away from the Indian, even as Johnny rode over to him.

"What's the matter?" Johnny said, for Billy wore a sour face. At first, Johnny thought maybe in the scuffle his brother had been stabbed, but Billy seemed unhurt. The Indian, though, was still prone on the ground, blood coming from his nose and his battered face red and scratched. His clothes were dirty and hung loose on his frame.

"He ain't even worth the fight," Billy spat. "Man's half starved. He ain't got no spirit in him."

Indeed, as he looked around, Johnny saw that the other Indians weren't offering any fight, either. They'd abandoned almost all the cattle. Three or four steers went over the top of the distant hill, having run at the sound of the gunfire. But the rest were milling about in the canyon – spread out but no longer moving with the Indians. The Indians were fleeing at a gallop, soon to overtake the few cattle that had started at the gunfire.

The others from the Townes Party were now rounding up the cattle, trying to push them back toward the wagons.

As fast as it started, it was finished.

Johnny Tucker killed the one he shot. The other one, the one Captain Walker shot, he would die too. He'd been hit in the gut and knocked from the horse, and he now writhed on the ground, uttering oaths in a language none among them understood.

"Go and fetch that pony," Billy said to his older brother, and Johnny rode up toward the Indian's horse and threw a rope over its neck. He brought the horse back to where Billy stood over the Indian. By that time, Elias Townes and Captain Walker had ridden over. Elias had told all the others to go and round up the cattle and get them moving back to the wagons, and they were doing that now. But the cattle were exhausted and moving slowly.

With Johnny holding the Indian's pony, Billy offered a hand to the man on the ground.

"Watch him," Captain Walker said. "He's got that knife on his belt."

"He ain't going for that knife, Captain," Billy Tucker said.

For a couple of moments, the Indian just stared at Billy's offered hand, but then he reached up and took hold, and Billy hefted him to his feet. Billy walked him a couple of steps to the pony and put the Indian's hand on the horse's side.

"Go on, now," Billy said. "We fought fair and you was licked. So go on now, and don't come back here."

Billy threw the rope off the pony's neck, and the bewildered Indian grabbed a handful of mane and hoisted himself up onto the horse's back. With a second look, he wheeled the horse to the far end of the valley and now fled in the direction the others had escaped.

"How come you did that?" Johnny asked.

"When I tackled him off that pony, I felt his ribs. That man is half starved," Billy said. "I could have punched him four or five more times and probably caved in his skull. But there ain't no honor in beating a man as hungry as that man is. Hell, if I was them, I have come to steal cattle, too."

"How come he's so hungry?" Johnny asked.

"Trappers and hunters and emigrants are killing all the game, or scaring off what they don't kill," Elias said. "Let's get these cattle moving before those Indians find some friends and come back and try to take them."

The cattle needed good water. All the livestock did. It was going to be a fight to keep them from drinking the poisonous water of the North Platte as they made the crossing. They'd probably lose some number of the steers in the crossing – maybe four or five. And here, these Indians were starving so bad that Billy Tucker wouldn't fight one. Elias had never known Billy Tucker to turn down a fight.

They left the dead man where he was, and the wounded one, too. If their friends wanted to come back and see to them, they could do that.

14

—— ◆ ——

ZEKE TOWNES MADE THE six miles or so down to the Devil's Gate and decided that would be as far as he would go this day.

At the Devil's Gate, he picketed the horses and explored the narrow notch, wide enough only for the river to pass. The canyon walls stretched straight up, imposing as they loomed over him. It was cool in the shade of the canyon, and Zeke took off his boots and rolled up his pants and waded through the cool, fresh water.

Towser splashed into the water, too, pouncing at it and then shaking himself violently. Dog and man both rejoiced in the fresh water, though Zeke felt a gnawing inside his stomach that was getting harder to ignore. He'd come far enough to solve his water problem, but he was running out of food with little hope that he would relieve his hunger before he got to Bridger's Fort. He still had two hundred miles or more to go. He had to make it through the South Pass and cross the Green River.

But now, he just wanted to revel in this moment. Fresh water in a gloriously beautiful canyon. In places along the canyon walls, pine trees had managed to take root and a few of them scattered through the notch grew straight and tall, their roots clinging to the side of the rocky walls. Down in the few spaces where the water did not reach from wall to wall and there was exposed dirt, a bright green grass grew thick, and Towser now was eating at a patch of grass. The river clear as glass cut through the canyon and over the rocky surface.

Big boulders of slate gray had cracked and fallen down into the river over the years, and especially up near the mouth of the canyon, the river turned white and frothy as it tumbled over boulders and dropped through a long shoal, splashing against rock, spraying into the air in a fine mist.

"What a grand adventure this is," Zeke said to the dog. "How many men will never see this? And here we are, splashing in this water, drinking as much as we can hold, and at least for right now, this is ours. We're the masters of the Devil's Gate. As troublesome as it's been, I'm blessed to have come on this journey."

Towser seemed indifferent to the words, but he snatched at some more grass and then barked at a little fish in the stream.

"I'd like to idle here forever," Zeke said.

But he knew that he could not. He collected a few pine branches from the ground, lucking into some dry ones, and walked through the cool water and over the sun-baked rocks out of the canyon where the horses were picketed on lines long enough to allow them to get down to the water. Duke and the bay were both drinking when Zeke came out of the canyon, but now they watched him as he dropped his load and sat down on a rock to put his socks and boots back on. He brushed the water and dirt from his feet, taking care to let the sun hit his feet to dry them as much as possible.

15

Neil Rimmer crossed his arms and gave his shoulders a small shrug. He said, "The way I see it, with all these folks moving out to Oregon Territory, there must be enough dupes and chawbacons out there around Oregon City that a man could live pretty well off the idiots for a long time."

Johnny Hubbard sucked his teeth.

"Well, you're a free man, Rimmer," Johnny Hubbard said. "You can go whichever way you choose."

"Cash me out," Rimmer said. "I'll sell my share of the scalps. And the other boys, too."

Hubbard frowned. Seven of them had decided to go with Rimmer. They were down in a camp at the foothills of the Winds, intending to follow the Little Sandy to the emigrants' trail and cut east from there, through the South Pass and along the Sweetwater River to Independence Rock. It wasn't that Hubbard had any objections to Rimmer and the others going west. It was their business. But he'd counted on having the full group of seventeen men. Anyone making the journey along the emigrant trail wanted more men than fewer. Whether it was dealing with obstacles or Indians, or just having enough folks along to kill off some of the boredom, Hubbard had thought seventeen was a good number. But now eight of them were going west.

The other thing Hubbard didn't like was cashing them out. In a journey of a thousand miles, one or two of them were bound to get thrown from their horse or drink some bad water. By the time they reached the Missouri River, Hubbard could easily expect their numbers to be a bit lighter, and when the time came to cash out, there would be a larger division of money for each man assuming some number of them died on the journey. But cashing out eight of them now meant the money had to be split among all seventeen, and if two or three didn't make it back east, the division would be smaller than it might have been.

"That's fine," Hubbard said. "We'll buy the scalps and cash you out."

"Ten dollars a scalp," Rimmer said, and Hubbard laughed.

"Not a chance," Hubbard said. "I'll pay five dollars a scalp, and that's generous."

"You'll get fifteen back east," Rimmer said through gritted teeth.

"We ain't back east," Hubbard said. "Injun scalps ain't worth a dollar here. Hell, I could turn around and go back up into them mountains and fetch twice as many scalps as we've got. The whole plains is littered with Injuns waiting on someone to come along and take their scalps. If you don't like it, I'll give you the scalps you lay claim to, and you can take them to Oregon City and sell them."

Rimmer had expected this. Hubbard would find a way to cheat him. He already knew it.

"Seven dollars," Rimmer said.

The two men continued to argue, Hubbard refusing to come off of five dollars, and Rimmer expecting more. Others, based on whether they intended to go west with Rimmer or east with Hubbard, joined the argument, and soon some harsh words were being exchanged.

Hubbard would have liked to put Rimmer down, and several times as the argument continued, Hubbard felt his fingers touching the grip of the knife on his belt. He didn't like Rimmer, particularly, and never had. He tolerated the man so long as their interests aligned, but now that they'd reached a diverging, Hubbard seriously considered putting an end to the argument by cutting out Rimmer's tongue through his neck.

"I won't be cheated," Rimmer said.

"Ain't nobody cheating anybody," Hubbard said. "This here is a fair deal. These scalps don't earn nothing here. If I'm toting them a thousand miles – risking my neck to do so – then I get paid for the risk."

"What risk?" Rimmer demanded.

"What if we come up on a band of a hundred Indian warriors somewhere down on the Platte?" Hubbard said. "They see these scalps, and then it's my scalp hanging on a lodgepole. That's a risk. You're trying to get paid for doing only half the work. And excuse me, but I saw you enjoying the work pretty well."

Rimmer snarled.

"Whether I enjoyed the work or not, that don't mean I did it for free."

"I ain't sayin' you did it for free. I'm sayin' you'll get paid here for what a scalp is worth here. If you want to take the scalps back east, you can get paid more. If you want to take the scalps to Oregon City and see what you can get for them, then you're welcome to do that."

Rimmer clenched his jaw.

He'd be happy to add Johnny Hubbard's scalp to the pile. Hubbard always wanted to be in charge, bark orders, and have everyone line up to do what he said. Rimmer never was that sort of man. He ran his own life without disruption from the outside. It was Hubbard's jawing that first made him think about maybe going west and trying his luck on the settlers rather than going back east.

"If I ever see you again, I'll know you as a no-account thief," Rimmer said.

"And if I ever see you again," Hubbard spat back, "I'll gut you like a fish and empty every drop of blood in your body."

Rimmer grabbed for his knife, and Hubbard grabbed for his. Every man in the camp stood on the verge of violence. But it was Johnny Hubbard who broke first.

"Hell, it don't matter," Hubbard said. "I'll give you seven dollars a scalp. Even if all we get for them back in Missouri is ten dollars a piece, we'll still come out ahead."

Some of the men started to laugh, relieved that there wouldn't be a fight. Others kept their fingers wrapped around the handles of their knives, just in case.

The sun had already broken and was now climbing across the sky. Johnny Hubbard sat in the dirt dividing out all the money – what they'd gotten from Bridger for the supplies they brought out and seven dollars for each scalp Rimmer and the others in his group had taken from the Indians. He had to dip into his share of Bridger's payments to buy the scalps, but it didn't matter. He knew every one of those scalps could fetch maybe fifteen or twenty dollars back East, and the farther east they took them, the more they'd be worth. Maybe in Baltimore they could sell a single scalp for twenty-five dollars. Not that Johnny would go so far. He'd sell them for ten dollars in Saint Jo or Saint Louis.

Hubbard finished dividing up the money with Rimmer watching over his shoulder. He handed two sacks to Rimmer for him and the other seven men going with him.

"It'll suit me fine if our paths never cross again," Hubbard said.

Rimmer grinned at him.

"It's a big ol' world, Johnny, but out here in the biggest parts of it, everything gets mighty small. I reckon we'll see each other again, and I won't forget you when we do."

"Yeah," Johnny Hubbard said. "I won't forget you, neither."

Hubbard and the others bound for the East watched as Rimmer and the seven going with him rode away, making tracks to the southwest toward Bridger's Fort. They'd ride more west than south until they came to the Green River, and they would follow that to the fort.

"We'll watch our backtrail for the next few days," Hubbard announced. "Until we're sure they've gone like they said they would. I wouldn't put it past them to try to catch us asleep in our camp and cut our throats to get the rest of this money."

"Maybe we ought to ride after them and cut their throats," one of the men suggested.

"Hell," Hubbard said. "Don't think I haven't thought of it. But we're better off letting them ride on this time. We need to make tracks east. We've got a long ride ahead of us, and we need to get it started."

16

ZEKE TOWNES PUT HIS nose to the air and gave a hearty sniff.

Smoke.

There could be no question about it. For the last half-hour he could smell it, smoke on the wind. Now the scent of it came stronger to him. He was riding toward someone, somewhere, who had a campfire going. His stomach rumbled. After weeks on the trail, he'd come to associate smoke with supper, and he wanted desperately to eat.

He scanned the horizon and saw nothing, no smoke or fire out on the barren prairie. But it was late in the day, he could turn and look back and see dusk catching up to him from the east. He might not see smoke in the waning light of the afternoon. And the wind whipped so hard across the South Pass that he might not see it anyway, every bit of smoke snatched and blown away.

But he could smell it.

Earlier in the day, Zeke had crossed the Sweetwater River for the last time. As Henry Blair had told him he would, he crossed the river and struck the South Pass without ever realizing it. According to the map Henry had given him, the South Pass was just beyond that last crossing of the Sweetwater River. But as he rode through the vast saddle, he saw no evidence that he'd reached the highest point on the

95

trail. Far off to the north and south of him, he could still see peaks rising infinitely higher.

But after some distance, the ground became more broken. Little valleys with steep escarpments eroded through generations. Small hills here and there.

There was no tree for shade nor to block the wind, and it blew like it had blown every second of every day since God first created the world and it would keep on blowing even if the world ceased to exist. Every time the wind snuck up under the brim of Zeke's hat, he'd have to throw a hand over the crown to keep from losing his only shade. The dog's hair ruffled in the steady breeze.

"You smell that, boy?" he called down to the dog. Towser sat on his haunches, sniffing the air the same as Zeke had done. "Is somebody roasting meat?"

The dog gave a chirp of a bark, as if answering the question.

"Well, hell, pup. Take me to 'em. Go find supper!"

The dog gave another bark and charged forward. Zeke gave a tug to the lead rope on the bay and pressed a knee into Duke's shoulder.

"Follow Towser," Zeke told the horse.

There were no hills to speak of. As Henry Blair had promised, the South Pass seemed flat as a pancake and wide as the sky. To the north, the peaks of the Wind River Range remained streaked in snow, at least in places, even in early July. From this distance, what he could see of them, Zeke understood Henry Blair's assertion that Oregon City would be unreachable if not for the South Pass. The mountains rose incredibly high, sharp slopes of solid rock and pyramid peaks – a wagon train could never cross them. And if all the mountains from the north to the south were like that, then certainly the South Pass must be the only way through.

Though worn with other worries, not the least of which was his own hunger, Zeke Townes longed to go to those mountains, to see them up close, to pass through the stream-torn crevices, to find the meadows and forests.

To the south, Zeke couldn't see any similar peaks, but he trusted Henry Blair that they were there. Mesas and buttes broke the horizon south and west.

But the flat land all around him had a roll to it, even though it seemed level as a board. Hollows and small rises in places succeeded in blinding a traveler to what might be only a mile in front of him, and the flatness of it all confounded that same traveler into believing a sweep of the eyes would take in everything for twenty miles. And everything for twenty miles seemed to be sparse grass and sagebrush.

But in fact, Towser now disappeared over the crest of a small rise, and his barking was such that Zeke knew the source of the smoke he could smell must be just a short distance beyond that rise.

Zeke rode directly into the wind now, and he had to reach up and hold his hat to keep it from whipping away. And as he topped the rise, now he saw ahead of him down in a shallow depression and maybe still half a mile ahead, a group of men and horses. The horses grazed lazily, some looking up now as Towser made known their presence. At first sight, Zeke's stomach gave a small lurch, the dread of coming upon a band of Indian warriors gripped him. But from their silhouettes he could see crowned hats with wide brims – these were white men, and he assumed them to be the first emigrants he'd seen since leaving his wagon train.

Everything was sparse grass and sagebrush. It seemed impossible to believe someone had found enough wood for a campfire, but they were certainly gathered as if they had a fire going. Coffee? Probably. Supper? Maybe.

Zeke took it easy, approaching the group slowly so as not to alarm them.

As he neared, and the silhouettes became distinguishable, Zeke understood how the men had accomplished a fire. He had thought they'd made their camp beside a large boulder. But now he saw it for what it was. Beside their camp was an old wagon, not dissimilar to the one Marie and Daniel traveled in. It was broken down and had been chopped apart for firewood. These men were not the first to come upon it and make use of its timber.

He counted something close to a score of horses and nine men. Towser didn't wait for an invitation to the camp, but bounded right in. One of the men put a foot out to keep the dog away, but another bent over and began to scratch him.

"Evening!" Zeke called when he was near enough to be heard over the wind, which meant nearly in the camp.

"It is an evening," one of the men called back. "Are you alone?"

"Just me and the dog. I'm riding for Bridger's Fort," Zeke said. "Mind if I come into your camp?"

"Come ahead, friend. If you've got a cup, there's coffee on the boil. We'll have supper cooking soon."

"Nice luck finding a wagon here," Zeke said, swinging a leg over the back of the gray horse and dropping from the saddle. He found the small effort made him dizzy, and he put a hand on Duke's back to steady himself. He didn't think any of the men noticed, though they were all eyeing him curiously.

"No luck in it. From here west, the entire trail is littered with wagons."

"From here west?" Zeke said. "Have you already been west?"

"We've been west, and our direction of travel is east," the man said.

"You're going back?" Zeke asked.

"Going back, but coming again next spring, My name is Johnny Hubbard. We're freighters. We brung supplies from Missouri early in the season and now we're headed for home."

"Tough way to earn a living," Zeke said.

"Not many easy ways to make a living," Hubbard said.

"My name is Zeke Townes."

Zeke held out a hand and Hubbard shook it. Some of the other men said their names or bid him good evening. The sun was dipping low and the light wasn't strong, but from what Zeke could see of the men, they looked like a rough bunch. He knew it wasn't fair to judge a man by the way he looked in the middle of a two-thousand mile trail, but even under the circumstances, these men looked rougher than most. Most of them wore thick beards and hadn't seen a barber in some time. Their clothes were a mismatched collection of homespun and skins. One man in the group wore a coat made from a quilt, and another used a length of rope for a belt. Some of them might have been Indians because breeches, shoes, and shirts were all made of skins.

"What puts you out here on your own, Zeke?" Hubbard asked.

Zeke didn't see any point in obfuscation. He told them the plain of it.

"I was traveling with a wagon train when we had a couple of teams of oxen get crossways with each other. Turned into a fight, and I stabbed another man."

"Huh," Johnny Hubbard said. "Killed him, did you?"

"Not on purpose," Zeke said. "And only after the other man struck me first."

"Banished?"

"That's how it is."

"I'm surprised you'd tell us all that," one of the other men spoke up. "Most folks'd come up with a story before they'd confess to killing and banishment."

Zeke shrugged.

"I figured it was better to say it now than let you figure it out for yourselves later," Zeke said. "If you don't want my company, I'd just as soon know it before I get the saddle off my horse."

Hubbard shrugged.

"You're welcome to eat with us and spend the night by our fire," Hubbard said. "I reckon there ain't a man here who can't name at least one place where he ain't welcome."

Another man in the group chuckled and said, "If your crime is killing, you've fallen in with the right company."

Johnny Hubbard drank liberally from a bottle. All of them did.

That afternoon, one of the men had shot an antelope, and they had more meat than they could eat. They shared with Zeke, and with Towser, too. The dog ate so much that he fell asleep early by Zeke's feet.

"What are your plans, Zeke?" Hubbard asked, the light of the campfire flames dancing across his face as he held out his bottle to his guest. Zeke waved off the liquor.

"Going to Bridger's Fort," Zeke said. "I'm hoping to find a wagon train that I can get on with there."

"They'd expect you to buy in," Hubbard said off-handedly. "You got money?"

"I don't," Zeke said quickly. "But I'm willing to work."

Hubbard chuckled.

"Everybody's willing to work. You'll find most of the wagon train captains still at Bridger's are going to want something more than another hand. Especially if you're begging for supplies."

"I can't resupply at the fort?" Zeke said.

"Not without any money," Hubbard laughed bitterly. "Old Gabe Bridger never learned the meaning of the word 'charity.'"

"Gabe? I thought his name was Jim Bridger," Zeke said.

"He's taken to calling himself Gabe lately. Can't say why. Anyhow, he ain't big on charity, and you'll find the prices at Bridger's Fort ain't Missouri cheap."

"Can't be much worse than the prices at Fort Kearney or Fort Laramie."

"Ha!" Hubbard scoffed. "You don't know Gabe Bridger. That man understands that when you got the only store for two hundred miles you can charge what you want."

"I reckon that doesn't surprise me," Zeke said, and he wanted to leave the subject of money behind. "Well, I don't have much choice but to go forward and try to find a wagon train."

"Where's the outfit you were with?" Hubbard asked.

"Behind me, still," Zeke said. "I figure they're still three or four days behind. Could be more than that."

"You got family with the wagon train?"

"I do. My wife and son. My brother is also with the train, and his family."

"How many wagons?"

"More than thirty," Zeke said, but he began to feel uncomfortable answering Johnny Hubbard's questions. Maybe it was all just idle conversation, but Hubbard's interest in the wagon train seemed suspicious. If he drove freight to Bridger's Fort every year, surely he'd seen enough wagon trains to lose interest in them.

"Mostly settlers? Families? Or is it working men in that train?"

"A little bit of both, but a fair number of army men who've decided to go west. A captain from the Seminole Wars down in Florida." Zeke had always thought of himself as an honest man, but he took the opportunity to lie. "I'd reckon half or better of the men in the train are all former army men."

"Is that right?" Hubbard said, and he seemed disappointed at the news.

"Where are the wagons you drove out to Bridger's Fort?" Zeke asked.

"Left 'em," Hubbard said. "Bridger wanted to buy our wagons, so we're just packing back to Missouri. Bridger can take them apart and sell the parts, or sell them whole. Or he can use them himself. It suits us fine. We can travel quicker on the way back to Missouri if we're packing. I reckon Bridger would buy the clothes right off our backs if we was willing to ride home naked. Any supplies are hard to get out here, and Bridger can double the price he'd pay in Missouri."

"We saw the prices at Fort Kearney," Zeke said.

"Well, like I said, Bridger's ain't cheaper," Hubbard laughed. "And there ain't as many supplies as what you found at Fort Kearney. Fort Kearney might as well be an Eastern port if you compare what Bridger has to what they've got there."

"Are there any wagon trains ahead? Any at Bridger's Fort?" Zeke said.

Hubbard shrugged his shoulders.

"Wouldn't know," he said. "We left Bridger's about a month ago."

"A month?" Zeke said, incredulous. Once he'd come upon this camp, he was certain he was not more than four days from Bridger's

Fort. Perhaps as few as two. And he'd thought the sustenance these men offered would be sufficient to get him to the fort. "Surely I'm not still a month from Bridger's Fort?"

"Oh, no. You could make it in maybe two days, maybe three, from here," Hubbard said. "But we left out of Bridger's about a month ago. Three weeks, anyway."

"Where have you gone that it's taken you a month to get this far?"

"We don't like to go back empty handed," Hubbard said. "If we're taking our wagons back with us, we load them up with skins or blankets or other trinkets the Indians sell at Bridger's Fort. Those things catch a fair price back East. But if we're packing back, we like to find a little village or camp of Indians and get some goods that are easier to transport."

"What goods?" Zeke asked.

"Show him," Hubbard said to one of the other men. In a moment, the man came back with what appeared to be a staff about four feet long adorned with a number of black feathers.

"What on earth?" Zeke asked, leaning forward for a better look. Not feathers. Small hides of some kind?

Hubbard chuckled.

"Injun scalps," he said. "Everybody east of the Mississippi wants to own one. These scalps is damn near better than going home with our pockets full of gold."

Zeke was confounded.

"Where did you get them?"

Hubbard laughed again.

"We made 'em out of beaver tails and twine!" he exclaimed, and pulled a laugh from those others around the campfire who were paying any attention. "Where do you think? We got 'em off the heads of Injuns."

Zeke drew back, revolted at the notion.

"You killed them?" Zeke said.

Hubbard continued to chuckle.

"We didn't want to, but they was all partial to their scalps and wouldn't give 'em up willingly."

There must have been fifteen or twenty of the scalps drying on the pole.

"We left out of Bridger's Fort and packed up into the Winds," Hubbard said. "Came across a winter camp of Shoshone. At least, we reckoned 'em to be Shoshone. Women, children, and old folks. The men was off on a spring hunt, we figured. A couple dozen of them in the camp, but some of them women sure put up a fight. Show him your gut, Winthrop."

One of the other men stood up and pulled his shirt from his britches and turned his body so that the firelight hit it. Indeed, he had a knife wound that went from the ribs on the right to the hip bone on the left. It was a vicious, deep wound, and still bore the stitches.

"She tried to gut me," the man called Winthrop said.

Zeke held his tongue. These men had fed him and his dog and offered him a fire to sleep near. As dizzy as he'd been getting down from Duke's back, they'd quite probably saved his life. But their boast over the scalps horrified him, and the callous nature of their laughing disturbed him equally.

"There's all sorts of ways we can make our trip more profitable," Winthrop said, but Hubbard – who was holding a stick he'd used to tend the fire, now swatted Winthrop's shins with the branch.

"What in hell was that for?" Winthrop howled, reaching down and grabbing hold to one his lower leg and then rubbing vigorously it to get the sting away.

"Just hush up," Hubbard said. "Our friend don't want to know about none of that."

"Sure I do," Zeke said, trying to quash the anger he felt rising in his chest.

"Abandoned wagons along the trail," Hubbard said. "That's all he means. Folks leave their wagons, and we can always find a few valuables to pick through. Maybe even come across some abandoned cattle down along the Platte."

Zeke grunted a response.

"I reckon I should turn in," Zeke said. "I'll want to make an early start for Bridger's in the morning."

"Yep. We'll get coffee boiling before sunup," Hubbard said. "Get some breakfast in you."

"I'm obliged to you," Zeke said.

All the same, Zeke never did more than doze through the night. He did not trust Hubbard and these other scalphunters enough to sleep well.

17

THE WAGON GAVE AN almighty lurch and dropped hard on the rock. Inside, something of glass shattered.

"Whoa!" Gabe Townes shouted.

"Hell and damnation!" Caleb Driscoll shouted, running forward.

Gabe was driving Marie Townes's wagon right in front of him, and he saw the entire incident but did not speak fast enough to stop it. Gabe wasn't paying attention, and the oxen led the wagon's wheel right up a rock. They might have been all right, but the wheel got too near the edge and dropped, and the axle fell hard against both rock and ground. With the sudden shudder of the wagon, the oxen stopped pulling – they didn't need Gabe to tell them to stop.

"We're lucky they didn't spook and stampede," Caleb said. "We might have had us a mess."

Jefferson Pilcher came running forward – his wagon behind Marcus Weiss's wagon.

"We do have a mess," Pilcher said, looking under the Townes wagon.

Fortunately, Marie and Daniel were both outside the wagon when the incident happened. They might not have been injured, but they'd have been jarred to hell and back. Marie leaned over to look, but she did not see what Jefferson Pilcher saw.

"What is it, Mr. Pilcher?" she asked.

"Busted axle, that's what," Pilcher said.

Word of any little trouble traveled along the wagon train quickly, and already the wagons ahead were beginning to stop. And Elias Townes was riding the palomino back toward the back of the train already. Gabe watched his father coming and felt a knot twisting in his stomach. A broken axle was truly a disaster. All of the wagons carried a spare wheel for front and back, but nobody had a spare axle.

"It's split, for sure," Caleb Driscoll said, getting down on his knees and having a look. "Split right where the axle goes into the thimble skein."

In just a matter of moments, it seemed, a dozen men were squatting beside the wagon, looking under it and offering their opinions.

"We could make a new axle from one of these cottonwoods," Jeff Pilcher suggested. "It'd take all day, but we could do it."

"Cottonwoods are too soft," Elias Townes said. "We need oak."

"We ain't plentiful on oak trees," one of the Tucker brothers said. "Maybe we can find a willow that's got a big enough trunk."

"Willow is no harder than cottonwood," Elias said. "Best we can do is cut down one of the cottonwoods and fashion two skids. Then strap them onto the frame of the wagon."

Henry Blair was among those now at the wagon, and he'd taken his turn looking under it at the broken axle. Henry now sucked his teeth and glanced up at the sky. Not only would they lose time in the work, but they were also going to slow down their rate of travel considerably.

"Be better to abandon the wagon altogether," Henry said.

"We cannot do that," Marie said quickly. "These are all our supplies. Everything we own is in that wagon."

Henry sighed. Folks were too quick to hang onto things. Later, when winter was coming fast or the terrain got too rough, most of these folks would start tossing out the things they now counted as precious. The whole trail was littered with people's most valuable items, held dear for too long and then left for good when conditions necessitated.

"It's your choice, Mr. Townes," Henry said. "I'm hired for advice. You make the decisions."

Marcus Weiss stood nearby and listened to the debate. He'd not offered an opinion yet, but nobody was surprised when he now interjected.

"The delay is too long," Weiss said. "Abandon the wagon."

"I don't need anything from you," Elias Townes said. "You've been aching to get at Zeke almost since we crossed the Missouri. You argued to get him banished, and now you just see another opportunity."

"No such thing!" Weiss cried out in his own defense. "But we are already risking the mountain snows if we do not keep moving. You cannot expect to put everyone in this wagon train in jeopardy to save one wagon and its contents."

Marie Townes appeared somewhere between the verge of tears and fury. Red faced, eyes watery. What was little Daniel supposed to do if they abandoned the wagon? Would the child walk to Oregon City? Not likely. Elias had made a promise to his brother, to get his wife and child safely to Bridger's Fort.

"That tree over there will do," Elias said, pointing to a cotton-wood. "Henry – you get the rest of the wagons moving. The livestock, too. I need a few men to stay back and help me. Everyone else can keep moving toward Bridger's Fort. We'll replace the axle there, and for now we'll just run it on a skid."

"I'll stay," Caleb Driscoll immediately volunteered. It was Caleb who had driven Zeke's wagon most of the way and then, after the incident between Marcus Weiss's man Fischer and Zeke, had taken over driving Weiss's wagon.

"You'll not stay," Weiss said. "You'll keep my wagon moving with the rest of the train. We lack good water, we're short on supplies. We've got to hurry to the fort, not waste time here repairing someone else's wagon."

Caleb shook his head.

"I said I would drive your wagon to Bridger's Fort," Caleb said. "And I'll get your wagon to Bridger's Fort. But I won't take orders from you, Mr. Weiss. If you don't like it, feel free to take the whip and take charge of your own wagon."

In a huff, Marcus Weiss took his family down by the river and they sat there waiting in the shade while a half dozen of the other men went to work cutting down a cottonwood and then shaping the trunk into two skids. It was hard work, but there'd not been many days yet that hadn't involved hard work. The other wagons and the men driving the livestock would go on, leaving just the few of them there.

Weiss was right, though, especially about the water. They'd gone beyond the fresh streams that carried decent water for drinking, and everything here was alkali. They needed to get on to the Sweetwater River where the livestock could again drink.

The wagons at the front of the train began moving, and the men herding the livestock in the cow column got the steers and oxen moving again.

Marcus Weiss's wagon remained behind, Caleb Driscoll helping to make the skids. Jeff Pilcher also stayed behind to lend his help. The others helping to make the skids were all packers – men who chose to make the journey with all their supplies packed on mule or horse. Most of these men helped in the cow column and pitched in when it came time to do the hardest work. Some of them pitched in because they were along as paid hands on the journey, but most of them helped because those with wagons provided them with meals and luxuries that a man packing all of his belongings couldn't bring with him.

While Elias led a group of them in cutting down a cottonwood and splitting it for the two skids, Caleb Driscoll and a couple others emptied Marie Townes's wagon, then piled rocks and boards under it to secure it. They removed the broken axle, salvaging the wheels and the iron skeins.

It was an all day job, and it wasn't long before the other wagons had disappeared from the horizon, gone over a rise. Caleb watched them for some time, when they were still visible, and then he watched the cloud of dust blowing across the horizon that showed where the wagons had gone. And then even the dust was gone.

"We'll be a day behind when we start, and losing ground every day after," Caleb said.

"I'll send riders back to check on you each day," Elias said. "When we get to Bridger's Fort, we'll find a replacement axle, or make one if we have to, and be ready for you there."

They lashed the skids onto each side of the wagon. Now, instead of wheels, the back of the wagon rested on two long, thick boards cut from the cottonwood trunk. It would drag rather than roll, and it would be slow going. Especially difficult on the beasts. Elias eyed the skids dubiously.

"If we were going much farther, I would be worried that the skids wouldn't make it."

"We'll be all right," Caleb said.

They'd kept back a spare team of oxen for each of the three wagons. But if they ran into serious trouble – another broken axle or an overturned wagon or illness, riders would have to come back from the main body of the wagon train to lend a hand.

Caleb got Marcus Weiss's wagon moving, and the Weiss family fell in alongside. Marcus, along with one of the packers, started the spare oxen moving.

Jefferson Pilcher followed behind with his wagon.

Elias took his son aside.

"Gabe, you do your best to keep up with Caleb. Watch where you're going and be careful."

"I will, Pa," Gabriel promised. "I'm sure sorry about this."

Elias shrugged his shoulders and sighed heavily.

"It ain't the first broken axle we've had, and it probably won't be the last. Just keep your mind on your job."

Gabe started the oxen moving. Daniel rode in the front of the wagon for a while, though on skids instead of wheels the jarring was much worse. Marie walked along beside the wagon, doing her best to stay on the shady side.

Elias walked Tuckee along for a ways, wanting to stay near to his son. He did not like leaving the boy back here so far from the rest of the wagon train. Young as he was, Caleb Driscoll was a good man, and he'd see after Gabe and Zeke's family. Still, Elias had misgivings. Any problem that came along, they'd have to deal with themselves. And while Elias trusted Caleb and Jeff Pilcher, he despised Marcus Weiss and mistrusted that man's motivations.

The sun already seemed eager to get below the horizon. Two hours of daylight left. Elias would be riding after dark to catch up to the main body of the wagon train.

"I've got to get moving," he said. "You just keep your nose pointed west, Caleb. Keep your mind on your job. I'll see you at Bridger's if I don't see you before, and I'll send back riders to check on you as I can."

Elias got Tuckee moving and caught up to Caleb Driscoll walking with whip in hand beside Marcus Weiss's oxen.

"Caleb, you've got about an hour before you'll have to stop and make camp for the night. I figure we'll out pace you, so you've got to keep these three wagons moving as best you can."

"I'll take care of everything, Mr. Townes," Caleb said. "You can count on me to look after Zeke's family and Gabe."

Elias touched the brim of his hat and gave his horse his head. He'd have a rough night catching up.

Jerry Bennett stayed back to help the three wagons left behind, mostly as another hand to keep the spare oxen moving. He and Caleb carried buckets of water up from the river to clean the oxen. Jeff Pilcher, with Gabe helping, gave them fresh water from the barrel on the side of his wagon. The four of them led the oxen off the trail a ways to find forage.

Marie made up a campfire, using sagebrush and a few cottonwood branches that Daniel had collected while the men made the skids. She would make rice and corn mush for supper, and cut some strips of bacon to help flavor the mush a little. Once she had the fire going, she stood and looked at the backtrail. She believed she could see the hill they'd gone over shortly after getting the skids in place.

"It's discouraging to look backwards and see the spot where you started the day," Marie said to Daniel.

For the boy, nothing was discouraging. He found it all to be such a grand adventure. Running over the prairies, sleeping on the bench inside the wagon, camping under the stars, eating his dinner off a campfire. Even the absence of his father did not seem to faze him. His father – Daniel was just like him. She wondered how much of this the boy would remember. Surely there would be parts of the trip that would stand out in his memory for the rest of his life. But he was so young – would they only be flashes of memory, a moment here and a moment there? Would he remember his father killing another man?

She tried not to complain too much in front of the boy, or to give voice too often to her discouragement. She did not want to sour whatever memories he might have, nor make the journey the more unbearable by sharing her own sorrow.

"Ma'am?" Gabe asked, walking up to Marie's fire.

"Oh, nothing," she said. "Just idle talk to Daniel."

"Yes, ma'am," Gabe said.

He still sometimes had trouble thinking of Marie as his aunt. She'd always been around, of course. She and Uncle Zeke had been inseparable when Gabe was growing up. It was like she was part of the family, but a part that didn't have a name. Of all of his father's siblings, Zeke seemed the most like an older brother to Gabe, and Marie was always there by his side. Their wedding simply made official what had always been.

"I sure am sorry about that axle," Gabe said. "I reckon I wasn't paying close enough attention."

"It's not your fault," Marie said.

Gabe knew different. He'd been day-dreaming, ignoring his work.

The three wagons weren't enough to form a circle large enough to corral the livestock, even with the falling tongues down, so they'd arranged the wagons to be points to a triangle, and Gabe and Caleb rigged up a corral using ropes tied to each wagon. After washing and watering the oxen and then taking them to graze, Caleb and Jeff Pilcher returned with the livestock and secured them in the makeshift corral.

Caleb and Jerry Bennett both ate their supper with Gabriel, Marie, and Daniel. It seemed natural as both Caleb and Jerry worked for the Townes family back in Tennessee and were bound for Oregon to work for them there.

After supper was finished and Marie was washing dishes, Jeff Pilcher went around, first checking on Marcus Weiss and his family, and then coming to Marie Townes's wagon to check on her group.

A heavy tension seemed to hang over the camp and the three wagons represented three distinct groups.

Jeff Pilcher's wife had been among the most vocal of the women speaking against Zeke, and neither she nor Marie had spoken a word to each other since Zeke's banishment. Marie likewise had no words for Marcus Weiss nor his family.

Back on the Platte River, at night when the wagon train stopped, several times many of them had heard Weiss abusing his wife. Marie tried to speak to the woman in private, but she refused the offers. Zeke had threatened Weiss, and the beatings stopped. Weiss still treated his wife cruelly, and he hovered over her in a way that prevented anyone from getting a private word with her. Luisa was her name. She was a frail woman with a pinched face that made her look much older than she was.

"Good evening, Miss Townes," Jeff Pilcher said as he came around. No one in particular had left him in charge nor suggested to him that he should be in charge, but other than Marcus Weiss, he was now the elder in the group, and Pilcher knew that Weiss would neither take it upon himself to check on the others nor do it in good faith if someone insisted that he should. So, at least in his own mind, Jeff Pilcher became the leader of the three wagon group.

"Hello, Mr. Pilcher," Marie said, the bite to her tone only just civil. "The evening has turned quite pleasant now that the sun is down."

"It has," Jeff Pilcher agreed. "I reckon the night will be chilly enough with that wind. I'm just checking that everything here is well."

"We're all fine, thank you," Marie said.

"It'll be slow going, but we'll get to Bridger's Fort a day or two after the others. Get this wagon fixed up, and then we'll be on for Oregon Territory."

Marie offered only a wan smile and a nod of her head.

Jefferson Pilcher stood awkwardly for several silent moments. He had liked Zeke and didn't enjoy seeing Marie's husband banished from the wagon train. He felt bad about the role he'd played in it, and that in part was why he decided to stay back with her wagon.

"Is there anything else, Mr. Pilcher?" Marie said.

"No, ma'am. Just let me know if you need anything," Pilcher said weakly.

18

"GOOD LUCK TO YOU, pilgrim," Hubbard said. "I wish you well making it to Bridger's Fort."

"I should make it, thanks to you," Zeke said. "I'm grateful to you for feeding me."

"Two days should get you there," Hubbard said. "Maybe three. You tell Old Gabe Bridger that you met us on the trail, and maybe he'll find some work for you."

"I'll give that a try," Zeke said.

"How far back do you figure your wagon train is?" Hubbard asked.

Zeke shrugged his shoulders.

"I couldn't say. I would expect you would come to them in four days. Maybe five."

Hubbard nodded his head thoughtfully.

"I wonder how many wagons are behind your group," Hubbard said.

"I wouldn't think many," Zeke said. "We got a late start back at Independence as it was. Anybody coming behind us will have to worry about the weather."

"That's true enough," Hubbard said. "But there's always one or two stragglers who push on even though they started too late.

They'll suffer for it. If we should encounter your family, should we give a message to them?"

"You can tell them you fed me and sent me on to Bridger's," Zeke said.

"We'll do that."

Hubbard and his men made a good breakfast of the antelope steak. There was plenty of meat, more than this group of men could eat, and they would leave what was left for the varmints because it wouldn't travel. As such, they did not mind sharing what they had with Zeke and with Towser. One of the men in Hubbard's group also gave Zeke some hardtack, and they spared a cup of coffee for him.

Zeke had slept with his guns beside him and his saddlebags as pillows for fear that these men would rummage through his belongings. But come morning, he was still in possession of all of his belongings. He'd even managed to hold onto the bag of coins his brother had given him, and when he bedded down that night he thought he'd likely lose the coins or lose his life.

Maybe Hubbard and the others believed him when he said he had no money. Or maybe they were not thieves and Zeke's fears were unfounded.

At any rate, he left their camp just after dawn, bound for Bridger's Fort, and Hubbard and his men were packing their gear and getting ready to set out.

Zeke rode out feeling rejuvenated. Bridger's Fort was a couple of days away, yet, but he had strength enough to make it, even if he didn't eat another bite of food.

As he rode, his thoughts turned to Marie and Daniel. Now that the ache in his belly was satisfied, he found a new yearning. He desperately missed his little family. He missed his brother, his nieces and nephews. He missed the company of the others in the wagon train. He chuckled to himself as he realized that he even missed Marcus Weiss's complaints.

"Well, maybe I didn't miss the man, but I reckon I miss hearing folks talk," Zeke told Towser.

The dog was keeping up this morning. Clearly the meal the night before and this morning had restored Towser's faith that Zeke was a worthwhile traveling companion.

He kept the horses to a walk, though. He saw no sense in destroying good horses just to try to get him to the fort a little faster.

"I think when the wagons reach Bridger's Fort, I'm going to take Elias up on his offer to split the wagon train," Zeke told the horses and the dog. "I don't mind telling y'all that information because I know you'll keep it to yourselves. But I can't go alone all the way to Oregon, and I don't like trusting strangers."

He glanced down at Towser, and though he knew the dog made no effort to offer an opinion, Zeke accepted the dog's glance as remonstration at his distrust.

"Yes," Zeke said. "I know that they fed us, and in your opinion that is the prime consideration. But those men murder for money. That's what those scalps were – people murdered so those men can sell their hair. What kind of man does such a thing?"

Even as he considered it, Zeke was disgusted with himself for having supper with them. An honorable man, he thought, would sooner starve than break bread with miscreants who murder women and children for their hair. Isn't that what they said? They struck on a camp where the men were off hunting and had only women and old people with which to contend. And what of those women? What treatment did they suffer before murder and scalping? Zeke shuddered to think of it.

Coming west, like any traveler, he knew that the Indians presented some danger, though he did not know to what extent. So far, the few Indians his wagon train encountered had been peaceful – even helpful. It sickened him to think that white men could be so cruel as to scalp a camp of women and old people just to be able to sell their hair back east, and it sickened him no less to realize there must be a market for Indian scalps.

And if these men were capable of such cruelty, what else might the be capable of?

Zeke thought about the questions they'd asked about his wagon train. He thought about his brother Elias encountering these men on the trail. Knowing Elias, he would invite them to supper. He might even let them camp among the wagons one night. And what atrocities would Hubbard and his men commit if allowed into the wagon camp?

Theft? Almost certainly.

Would they defile a white woman in a wagon train? Probably, if the opportunity presented.

Were these the types who would run off livestock? Zeke did not doubt it. They might cut out a few steers to help them get back east.

And if an objection was made, would Hubbard and his men turn their guns on the Townes Party? Possibly they would.

With a heavy sigh and a thought to how hungry he'd been the day before, Zeke Townes drew reins and sat for several long moments.

Everything as far as he could see to the west was sagebrush and hard-packed earth. To the south, there was nothing to be seen except the horizon. Even as he twisted around and looked back to the east, Zeke could see nothing of the hundreds and hundreds of miles he'd already come, nothing of the Platte River valley, nothing of the green, grassy plains of Kansas, nor even the bluffs of the Missouri.

The Mississippi and the Ohio did not exist behind him, nothing but sagebrush and dry, hard-packed earth, the sort of soil that did not give a man hope.

To the north stood the Wind River Mountains, just a thin line of blue and white on the horizon. Zeke frowned at the Winds – they were the only reminder that a world existed that was not flat and covered in sage. No tree. No bush. Nothing to break the monotony.

Ahead of him, somewhere beyond his ability to see, Zeke knew there was the Green River, and it would need to be crossed. And then, some eighty miles down the trail, Bridger's Fort.

He could press on. He could make it to the fort, and there he would find sustenance, water to drink, a warm bed at night.

But behind him drove a wagon train where he was not wanted and could not go for help. But in that wagon train rode his wife and son, his brother – all the family he would ever have again in his life.

And if Zeke's intuition was right, those people were in danger.

19

THE HORSEMEN CAME LATE in the day, catching Zeke Townes with the sun in his eyes.

Up ahead a short distance was a what he'd taken to be the Big Sandy River, and it was from the banks of the river that the horsemen appeared.

The first he knew of them, they were almost on top of him already. They rode small ponies and moved fast, fearsome in their swiftness.

He'd been watching his backtrail all through the day, counting himself lucky that he did not see Hubbard and those other men on the eastern horizon. By late afternoon, he'd stopped watching quite so much, satisfied that no one rode behind in pursuit. He even laughed to himself and joked with Towser how angry Hubbard would be if he knew he'd missed a hundred dollars in coin.

But he expected no trouble from ahead.

How they managed to get so close without him ever seeing, Zeke would never know. The first rider came up from a hollow with the sun directly at his back. Zeke had to blink a couple of times to even be certain he saw a rider there. But then there were others, maybe a dozen of them. Maybe more. They came waving spears and shouting a banshee's call. Zeke's blood turned to ice as sight passed to understanding and he came to realize that it was an Indian attack.

He'd heard the Indians were all mostly friendly along the trail. Back in Missouri, they'd said travelers should take supplies to trade with the Indians. The biggest worry was that some might raid a wagon column with the intention to cut out some livestock. But they wouldn't harm travelers unless provoked.

All the same, Zeke had come up with stories of Indians scalping white men, burning villages, raping women, and it was the fear of his childhood that gripped his heart now.

He grasped the grip of his saddle gun and wrenched it from its leather holster, but he never even managed to cock back the hammer and release the trigger.

His shoulder took the brunt of the blow from the war hammer, but the heavy weapon glanced off the shoulder and struck Zeke in the side of the head. Immediately he went dizzy. The whole earth began to spin. Duke panicked and started to run, but one of the horsemen who'd ridden up to him grabbed the bridle and held the horse.

Zeke's head spun around and around, dizzying. No clear thought formed in his mind, and sky and land blurred together.

Another man grabbed Zeke's shirt at the back and twisted it into his fist, then wrenched Zeke from the saddle, dropping him to the ground. Zeke felt the gun come loose of his grasp.

There were men over him now, angry and shouting, shaking their spears. Their faces looked like the faces of demons. Their bodies, half naked, painted and horrifying, muscles bulged from small frames. Fists and feet, beating and stomping.

"I can't understand you!" Zeke shouted, but his voice sounded feeble. He had no strength to fight and wasn't sure how long he'd even stay conscious.

The words they shouted back were foreign and terrifying, and one of the men kicked him hard in the ribs. The best Zeke could manage was to try to curl himself into a ball.

He had some vague thought that Marie and the others would find him here, his body mutilated. He wished they would take him someplace else, someplace away from the trail. Better that she would never know if never knowing spared her the sight of his hair cut from his head, his insides pulled all out, and whatever other terrible thing these savage men might do to him.

As some of them continued to shout at him and smack him with their spears or kick him or punch at him, Zeke knew others were stripping his horses. Saddle and pack, flung to the ground. The contents of the pack being tossed all over. Elias's hundred dollars in the hands of Indians who didn't know a coin from a skipping stone.

One of the men grabbed him up from the ground, holding him by his shirt. Another slapped him hard, and they dropped him back down. Zeke waited in absolute terror for one of those spears to pierce his guts or for the blades on their belts to start hacking at his scalp.

Everything was terrible chaos, and Zeke could see the men tossing his belongings.

Again, a hammer crashed into the side of his head, and Zeke felt the world slip away from him as his vision failed.

Marie Townes stroked her son's hair as he slept on the ground beside her. They'd made up a pallet under the wagon and Daniel had fallen asleep trying to count the stars, as he had so many other nights on this journey.

She couldn't say why, but this night she felt particularly distant from her husband. Ever since his banishment, she'd been able to feel his presence on the trail ahead. A rock that caught her eye, she knew he'd come past that rock. The bright blue sky overhead, she sometimes felt he was looking up at it the same as she was, in the same moment, separated but both of them looking at the same blue sky. She felt the same with the sunsets, these glorious sunsets that filled the entire western horizon. In the mornings, when the sun cracked the eastern darkness, she wondered if Zeke was just opening his eyes the same as she.

But this night, she could not feel his presence. This night she could not look up at the stars and feel him looking at them, too.

"Oh, Zeke," she said softly, speaking to herself so as not to disturb the boy. "May God watch over you and keep you close. My only hope for our lives together rests in Him."

In the morning, even before the sun was up, the men grazed the livestock before getting the oxen harnessed and beginning the journey. Marie and Daniel started the day walking beside the wagon, following behind Gabe as he called to the oxen, pulled the harness, and waved his whip. It was more of the same, how they'd spent every day. One foot and then the next. One mile and then the next. The only real evidence that they moved not in vain was the growing distance from the spot where they'd camped. The only evidence that time passed from one moment to the next was the sun's movement in the sky.

With the sun now overhead, Caleb Driscoll called back to the others.

"There's riders ahead!"

Even as he said it, Marie saw the riders – who'd been at a walk – kick their horses into a gallop.

Caleb fetched a rifle from the back of Weiss's wagon, and Jeff Pilcher came running past with his own rifle in hand. The oxen kept moving. The wheels of the wagons continued to turn. Jerry Bennett drew a saddle gun from its holster, but he did not stop the livestock.

Marie put her hands on Daniel's shoulders and moved the boy with her to the back of their wagon, but they did not stop walking.

Pilcher ran ahead of the wagons maybe fifty or sixty yards and then he stopped, his eyes on the approaching men. Then he turned and waved his hat.

"It's Henry Blair!" he shouted, and Caleb Driscoll took up the message and shouted it back.

Marie watched as the riders dashed directly past Pilcher. There were three of them, but she recognized Henry Blair at the front. Blair rode past Weiss's wagon and pulled his reins as he approached Marie and Daniel. Billy and Johnny Tucker were the other riders, and they galloped up right behind Blair and also reined in.

"Ma'am! I have a message from Elias that he asked me to give to you," Henry said, panting. Marie's heart sank, for she knew that Henry must have been sent back with some awful news. He checked over his shoulder to be certain that Caleb Driscoll was in earshot. "The main body of the wagon train has come to Independence Rock!"

Marie furrowed her brow.

"Is that good news?" she asked.

"Exceptional good, ma'am," Henry said, a wide grin pained across his dusty face. "It's fresh water. The Sweetwater River runs there beside the rock dome. But better than that, and this is what Elias wanted you to know – we came upon the rock before sundown yesterday, and some of us clumbed it to the top."

"You clumbed it, Mr. Blair?" Marie asked.

"Indeed we did, ma'am, and there on the top we found an engraving!"

"An engraving?"

"It's common, ma'am, for travelers on the trail to leave their mark up on that rock. And when we clumbed it, we found there Mr. Zeke's 'scription. It says, 'Zeke Townes, July of 1846.'"

"Oh, thank Heaven," Marie said. "He's passed that way ahead of us."

"Yes, ma'am. He's still up there moving ahead."

"Praise the Lord," Marie said, and she gave Daniel's shoulders a small shake. "Your papa, Danny."

Henry wheeled his horse now and spoke to Caleb, ignoring Jeff Pilcher and Marcus Weiss.

"Mr. Elias says to press on – through the night if you must. He says you'll need to water the livestock. But be careful as you get near. Them oxen is gonna smell the water, Caleb, and they'll charge if you ain't on top of them."

"Is Mr. Townes waiting for us ahead?" Caleb asked.

"They spent the morning watering livestock, refilling barrels. But he intended to get moving by noontime," Henry said.

"Can we be there by sundown?" Pilcher asked.

Henry wrinkled his face and wiped sweat on his forearm. He checked the sun's position in the sky as he did his reckoning.

"I doubt it, Mr. Pilcher," Henry said. "But maybe not too late after dark."

Even while they spoke, the wagons continued to move. Caleb and Gabe seemed to find a way to quicken the pace.

Henry Blair looked back to Marie.

"Is all well here, ma'am?" he asked.

"Much better now, thanks to your news."

20

Johnny Hubbard ran the sharpening stone up the blade of his knife and watched Winthrop lick his fingers after flipping one of the steaks on the fire.

Hubbard had seen a deer at dawn and managed to track it a little ways. He shot it down near the Sweetwater River. It was good luck to have fresh meat twice up here, and he thought of it as a sign that they were going to have good luck the entire way back to Missouri.

"Wish we had time to smoke some of this meat for the trail," Winthrop said.

"No time for that," Hubbard said. "Until we get some ways down the Platte, I'll still be nervous about them Injun bucks from that camp where we took them scalps."

"They won't be no trouble to us," Winthrop said. "I bet it'll be a week or longer before they're back to their camp. And then what use is it to them to try to follow us?"

Hubbard chuckled and gave his knife a good long stroke with the stone.

"If they do come back and come after us, maybe they'll light on Neil Rimmer's trail and get his scalp."

"It won't be a problem one way or t'other," Winthrop said. "But we do have something to consider."

"What's that?"

"That feller that camped with us a couple nights back. He says there's a wagon train in front of us somewhere. What do we do about that?"

Hubbard nodded his head.

"He said they was full o' army men."

"You believe that?" Winthrop said.

"He had no reason to lie."

"Unless he took the measure of us. You was pressing him hard about them wagons. Maybe he got suspicious of all your questions."

Hubbard shrugged his shoulders.

"I don't reckon we'll do anything with that wagon train," Hubbard said. "Less the ones that went with Rimmer, we're down to ten men now. Not hardly an outfit that should take on an entire wagon train. He might've been lying about how many in the train are military men, but they'll have some boys among 'em who are game enough. In the cow column, I'd reckon."

"Uh-huh. And it don't take much for a man to load a rifle and pull a trigger," Winthrop agreed. "If they're bound for Oregon, they'll be family men, most of 'em. Family men'll always make a stand. Even if we kill 'em all, I suppose we'd lose some number. Maybe four or five of us."

"And then it's hell getting back. The fewer of us there are, the harder it'll be to make it back to Missouri."

"Maybe we'll run across some stragglers," Winthrop said. "Be nice to have a wagon or two for the trip back."

"Wagon would just slow us down. We'll be back to Missouri a mite faster if we pack the whole way."

"But a wagon means supplies. Coffee and sugar. Probably some dried meat. Blankets on a cold night. Might even have some valuables worth toting back east."

"Slow us down," Hubbard said again. "I'm ready to get back to St. Jo."

"If there's a straggler, we should think about it," Winthrop said.

Hubbard cut his eyes in Winthrop's direction. He'd already suffered one mutiny on this return trip, and he didn't like the idea of another. Rimmer was no great loss. He was a troublesome man, argumentative and ill-tempered. And any one man, even Winthrop, didn't matter much one way or another. But they'd lost seven men with Rimmer's treachery, and if another seven decided to follow Winthrop, Hubbard would have a decision to make. Three men couldn't make this journey on their own. Either Hubbard would have to acquiesce to Winthrop's whims and through that show of weakness possibly lose his position in the group, or he'd have to cut Winthrop's throat. Winthrop was weakened from that slice wound, but he'd still be hell in a fight.

"If there's a straggler, and they're far enough back that the others won't hear the shooting, we can talk about it," Hubbard agreed. "But the conditions must all be right. If it puts us in jeopardy, we shan't do it."

Winthrop shrugged.

"We'll see what it's like when we come across it," he said.

Hubbard nodded at the fire.

"Them steaks just about ready?"

Winthrop stabbed one of the steaks and lifted it from the rock where it was cooking. The blood on the rock, surrounded by hot coals, sizzled as he lifted up the venison steak.

"Still a mite pink, I'd say."

"Keep cooking it," Hubbard said.

He didn't like the bargain he'd struck with Winthrop. One thing for sure, if you came across a wagon train this far out, there was bound to be a straggler or two. Sometimes a train of sixty wagons would be spread out for fifty miles. The first and last wagons might not even remember that they were of the same party. Illness. A broken wheel. Escaped cattle. A difficult water crossing. A missing child. Anything could delay one or two wagons, and anything else could delay two or three more. Pretty soon, one big wagon train became a tail of delayed wagons. Usually they would travel in small groups, three or four here, five or six there.

With ten men, they couldn't handle more than four or five wagons. But if they could approach friendly-like, maybe share a supper, then they could set on them. Take the men first. Hubbard and his outfit could handle a score of men if they could get close to them, and they could probably do it with knives, mostly. Maybe only a couple of shots, but not enough to raise suspicions among the main group of wagons. If the conditions were right, Hubbard decided, they could do it. Grab a wagon for the journey home, load it with supplies to make the traveling easier. Maybe it would add a week or so to their travel time. They could do with more horses, anyway.

But the conditions would have to be exactly right. Something fewer than five wagons, strung out well behind the main body of wagons. And not a lot of men to contend with. This trip had been successful up to now, even with Rimmer leading off a group of men. Hubbard didn't care for the thought of nursing a festering wound all the way back to Missouri.

21

ZEKE TOWNES'S SKULL THROBBED, and it took some effort to shake off the lethargy.

He woke to confusion, not certain of where he was or what day it was or how he came to be here in this place. His confusion compounded by the pounding in his head. He knew instinctively he'd taken a beating, even before his brain took the measure of his hurts. He knew, too, that the sun was well up in the sky, though his eyes burned from the light and he'd not yet checked to see how high. He guessed rightly that it must be mid-morning.

He rolled from his back and lifted his arm up to shield his face, and only then did he open his eyes. He heard Towser panting nearby, and his movement must have roused the dog. Towser came over and stuck his nose into the open space that Zeke's arm formed, and the dog started licking his ear.

"All right, Towser," Zeke said, reaching out his arm to hold back the dog and give him a gentle scratch at the same time.

Then the memories began to come. The Indians, vicious and brutal.

But they'd left him alive?

His hand moved to his own hair, and Zeke was surprised to find it there.

He sat up now and stripped out of his shirt and looked himself over. He was bruised up pretty good. His ribs and upper arms bore green and blue marks.

"They did a number on me," Zeke told the dog.

He ran a hand over his face and felt the dried blood on his cheek. His hair on the side of his head was matted with blood, and there was an egg about the size of Towser's paw protruding from above his ear.

"Damn good number on me."

His things were scattered all around. Saddle and pannier tossed haphazardly onto the ground. Shirts and undergarments. His blanket. The trail guide Henry Blair had given him.

Those Indians who rode up out of the sun and set on him with such swiftness and violence had left Zeke Townes with his life, which was quite a bit more than he'd expected. But it wasn't all they'd left to him. They'd left his guns and his knife, his powder and his ammunition. The things he would have expected them to take even if robbery hadn't been the motive for the attack. He found the bag with the coins that Elias gave him. The coins spilled out, though he found all of them in the dirt. But Indians put no value on Anglo coins, at least not out here in the prairies and mountains.

In the distance, he saw that they'd left even more. There he could see Duke and the bay.

"What was the point?" Zeke asked out loud. "Why rush me like that if they weren't even going to take my horses?"

Battered and sore, Zeke saw first to his own survival. He could not find a rope – one of the two things it appeared the Indians did take – so he started across the open prairie with empty hands to try to collect the two horses. As he approached Duke, he could see plainly that the bridle was still on the horse's head and the reins hung loose in front of him. Zeke took up the reins and gave them a small tug, but Duke was always an easy horse to catch. The bay was less interested and deliberately wandered away as Zeke and Duke approached, but eventually he allowed himself to be caught as well. He had no reins attached to his harness. When the Indians attacked, Zeke had been leading the bay with the missing rope.

With both horses in tow, Zeke returned to his scattered belongings. He found a cloth that seemed mostly clean and led the horses down toward the river. It was about a mile ahead of him. He dropped Duke's reins and gave the bay a stern command to "stay put," for all the good that might do. Then he went down to the river bank and plunged the cloth in.

He guessed this was the Big Sandy River, though he couldn't know for sure. If so, he wasn't more than a hundred miles now to Bridger's Fort.

The water against his head was cool and brought some relief to the pounding. He couldn't see enough of his face reflecting in the surface of the water to scrub himself well, but he did try to get some of the dried blood off the side of his head. He could feel where it had crusted all the way down the side of his neck.

He'd been unconscious overnight. For all he knew, it could have been two nights and a day, except he wasn't sun burned, which he would have expected if he'd lain out there exposed all through a day.

The horses lapped some of the water, standing on the bank, and Towser stayed nearby, surely wondering about breakfast.

When he'd done what he could to wash his face, Zeke dabbed the water at the side of his head. The slightest touch sent electric shocks of pain through his skull, but he was grateful to still have his hair.

And that thought led to another.

He remembered the scalps drying on the pole that the man Winthrop had showed him.

What were those Indians looking for? A scalp, maybe? Were these the braves who returned to their summer camp in the Wind Mountains to find their women, their elderly, and their children all massacred for their scalps so that Hubbard and those others could sell Indian hair back east? Were these warriors on the trail of Hubbard and the others?

Zeke couldn't hardly muster a bit of sympathy for Hubbard and his crew. They'd taken to murder for profit, and if they received the just deserts from that life, then Zeke wouldn't shed a tear on their behalf. He'd been sickened by the sight of the scalps, all drying on a pole. He couldn't fathom the horror the Indians had felt at returning to their camp and finding their families murdered and scalped.

Nor could he hardly blame those warriors for the treatment he'd received.

What if he came back to the wagon train from a hunt and found Marie and Daniel murdered for their scalps? Wouldn't he ride in pursuit of vengeance? And wouldn't he offer ill treatment to anyone he encountered who might've been responsible?

The trail offered a stern code for the men who followed it, and all men who made their life along the trail had to abide by that code. Justice and vengeance often became one and the same.

Zeke's attitude might have been different a day or two ago, but he couldn't shake from his mind the terror he'd felt when those Indian warriors all surrounded him and pressed around him, and his thankfulness at being left alive purely from the mercy of the men who attacked him made him see things in a more philosophical way.

They'd cut the cinch tie strap from his saddle, the Indians had, and Zeke had to use his knife to poke fresh holes through the leather.

He found his piggin strings from his saddle bags and used those to bind the strap. A makeshift repair job, but it would serve to get him to Bridger's Fort.

22

THE TOWNES PARTY HAD stopped their wagons about an hour ago, and it was now dusk.

Elias Townes left them to the work of setting up camp for the night. They all knew their roles well enough. There were days now when Elias had trouble remembering any life previous to life on the trail. Saddle the horse. Ride a ways. Walk a ways. Settle some minor dispute among the emigrants. Work like a dog at a river crossing or an embankment. Truth of it was, there were days when Elias hoped for some trouble along the trail just to break the monotony. He'd heard of places where wagons had to be unloaded and lowered down cliffs by rope and pulley. They'd yet to encounter such a thing, but some mornings Elias woke with the hope that there would be some such obstacle so that they might enjoy some new distraction.

Even the sights had grown old. The mountain peaks, the fantastic rock formations, these things that had been new and incredible when first beheld, now held little interest. One range of peaks on the horizon was very much like any other range of peaks on the horizon. Granted, the Devil's Gate and Independence Rock were a thrill to see, but less for their impressive formations than for the days of anticipation, the eagerness to see them. Chimney Rock had been something to see, prominent on the western horizon for days, and then on the backtrail's horizon.

He rode now back the way they'd come, making for a prominent cluster of rocks that would give him an advantage to see what was behind them.

They'd lingered back at Independence Rock and at Devil's Gate. All the folks of the party wanted to get a look at the place where the Sweetwater had cut such an impressive gap. There'd been time, too, in crossing the Sweetwater below Independence Rock and then crossing back to the north side of the river when they'd gotten beyond Devil's Gate.

Elias had hoped that Caleb Driscoll leading Marie, Weiss, and Pilcher might have gained ground on them during those delays. He'd not sent riders back to make certain that the small group of three wagons had made it back and forth across the river, and now he was wishing he had. He just wanted to know that they were fine and still on the trail.

He dropped Tuckee's reins and left the horse with a ground tie, and he climbed to the top of the rock outcropping. He had no need to shade his eyes, for the sun was at his back, but still a hand went up as if by instinct to the front of his hat.

Elias Townes saw nothing on his backtrail. No cloud of dust nor any other evidence that his brother's wife and son were still behind him.

Marie's wagon would be slow on skids. Elias did not know what difficulty it would cause in the water crossings, though he'd found neither of them to be difficult in the least.

He waited perhaps a half hour and looked again. Still nothing but the dark of day in obvious pursuit. Then he gave up. Likely, they'd stopped for the night already and would not appear on the horizon even if he stayed here until sunset.

Now he climbed back down the outcropping and took up his reins. Squinting through the glare of the setting sun, Elias could see the wagons ahead, already forming a large circle. The Tucker brothers and Henry Blair and some of the other men would be spreading the livestock out now, going north of the trail to find good forage. The womenfolk would already have fires going and suppers cooking. Elias felt a rumble in his own belly.

He walked beside Tuckee, leading the horse, feeling his hot breath against the side of his neck. Elias put out a hand and rubbed the horse's shoulder.

"One day you'll be proud in the knowledge that you've walked a good bit farther than most horses have," Elias said to the palomino.

He was idly walking, not giving much thought to anything other than the concern he had for his sister-in-law, when he saw something beyond the camp. His first thought was that he'd seen some of the cow column returning with the livestock, but what he saw came from the west, farther west than the cow column would have gone.

Go-backers? Maybe, but not likely. Who would get this far along the trail and decide now to turn back? He was looking at maybe a score of horses with half of them carrying riders.

Indians determined to steal some cattle? This seemed most likely.

Townes quickly mounted and gave the palomino a tap with his reins to get the horse moving. Tuckee was quick to the gallop, and Townes shouted ahead to alert the others, waving a hand and pointing. As he neared the camp of circled wagons, he saw some men had rifles and were going out to meet the threat that appeared from out of the west. Others, some of them from the cow column, rode back now, and they got to the wagons about the same time as Elias.

As he rode up, he searched for his own wagon in the circle and now made directly for it. Tuckee had hardly come to a halt when Townes dropped from the saddle and hurried to the wagon. He gave a glance over his shoulder and saw that the riders were fast approaching now, but he also saw that they were not Indians at all, but white men on saddled horses and toting pack horses.

Captain Walker approached, armed with a rifle and walking at a quick pace.

"Who could it be?" the captain wondered aloud.

"Indeed," Elias said. "I cannot imagine. Surely not go-backers from this far out."

Some of the other men now were gathering nearby. Among them were Johnny Tucker, mounted, and Reverend Marsh and Noah Bloom. Noah had a rifle in his hand and a knife on his belt, but the pastor came unarmed.

"I'm going to ride out and see who they are and what they want," Elias said. "Captain Walker, you might want to gather up some of the men and prepare a defense. Just in case."

"I'll do it."

"I'll ride with you," Johnny Tucker said.

Elias did not object. If these men were trouble – thieves or scavengers or an outfit of wanted murderers – Johnny Tucker would only prove to be so much help. But company was always welcome in times of danger.

Elias mounted the palomino, and the two men rode out, keeping the horses to a walk.

"You have your saddle gun?" Elias asked.

"I do."

"You keep it present to your hand. And you ride a few feet behind me. If they show trouble, let them show it to me first."

They met the approaching riders about a quarter of a mile out from the camp. The men looked weary, covered in dust, but they came with their hands empty. One of them gave his horse a kick and rode out in front of the others.

"How-do, pilgrim," he said.

"I'm all right," Elias said, a glance over his shoulder to see that Johnny Tucker had stayed back a few feet.

"My name is Johnny Hubbard. I'm a freighter, just come from Bridger's. You bound for Oregon City?"

"I am."

"You must have a son called Zeke," Hubbard said.

"I have a brother called Zeke."

Hubbard chuckled.

"Sure. You're too young to be his daddy, I reckon. Brother, huh? Well, about three nights ago, we camped with your brother and he said you was coming up behind."

"Is that right?" Elias asked, feeling slightly more at ease than he had before.

"Zeke asked us, if we ran across you, to let his wife know that he's healthy and making for Bridger's."

"If you're freighters, how come you ain't hauling wagons?" Johnny Tucker asked.

"Sold 'em to Bridger. We're packing back."

"Zeke's eating okay?" Elias asked. "How's his health?"

"He was fit and in a good state. We fed him well," Hubbard said. "We had antelope. Winthrop! Wasn't it antelope that night Zeke Townes was with us?"

A man back with the others called back, "It was antelope that night."

"How far out is he from Bridger's Fort?" Elias asked.

"He could be there now, or in another day, so long as he wasn't slowed down none crossing the Green River," Hubbard said.

The words came as a gift to Elias Townes, wracked with guilt over the sending off of his brother. To know that these men had seen Zeke and found him in good health brought Elias tremendous relief.

"I wish his wife was here to take the news from you herself," Elias said.

A dark cloud passed over Hubbard's face.

"She didn't make it?" he asked, taking his hat from his head and clutching it to his breast in a show of deep sympathy.

"Oh, no!" Elias said. "It's not like that. She's just not up with the wagon train."

Hubbard quickly returned his hat to his head.

"You ought not to let women wander alone."

Elias chuckled.

"No, that's not it, either. Her wagon has a busted axle. She and a couple others from our party are behind us some distance, but coming on still. The rest of the train kept moving. We're planning for her to rejoin us at the fort where we can repair the axle."

"Is that right?" Hubbard said. "Foul luck, that. You have a sizable party stay back with her?"

"Two other wagons," Elias said. "I'd hoped that they might catch up to us at the river crossings, but we've got the one wagon running on skids, and I reckon they're just that much slower."

"Well, that should be fine, then. They're rejoin you at Bridger's and you can have a new axle waiting."

"That was our thinking," Elias said. "I'd be proud to have you men join us for supper and make camp with us, if you care to. We're light on supplies, but I'm sure we could repay you the kindness you showed to my brother."

Hubbard shook his head.

"No, thank you, though. That's kind of you, but we won't trespass on your supplies when we have our own. We've had a run of good fortune. An antelope three or four days back and a mule deer yesterday. We's well fed. But we might bed down below that ridge, there. Camp nearby, if you don't mind."

The men made fires from sagebrush and juniper from down near the river bank. They made up biscuits and fried bacon and ate as the sun made its final plunge under the western horizon.

"Three wagons are separated from the main body of the wagon train," Hubbard said, keeping his voice down.

He and Winthrop sat on rocks facing the wagon train camp not two hundred yards from their own camp.

"They told you that?" Winthrop asked.

Hubbard chuckled.

"Ol' Zeke's brother told me that," Hubbard said. "I reckon it put him at ease seeing as how me and Zeke are such good pals."

Winthrop nodded.

"So delighted to get news of his banished brother that he didn't even guard his mouth."

"Uh-huh."

"So what do you think?" Winthrop asked.

Hubbard thought of the antelope and the mule deer. He thought of the Indian camp with the men all gone. He thought of the good bargain they'd made with Bridger. He couldn't have asked for a more profitable journey. They'd gotten out here early in the season and found Bridger in need of supplies and willing to pay. They'd added to their bounty with Indian scalps. And now they had the opportunity to do one more. Three wagons straggling behind the others. There wouldn't be but a handful of men with those wagons. They could approach them the same as they'd come at Elias Townes, bearing news of the woman's husband. Zeke Townes's wife would likely invite them in. Have supper with us, she would say. You're welcome. Tell me more about my banished husband.

"I think it'll be easy pickin's," Hubbard said. "If you want to take one of those wagons, see what they've got that might be worth taking back, I won't object to doing it."

Winthrop nodded.

"Be nice to have the comfort of supplies on the trip home. If they've got money or valuables, it just makes it that much the better."

"Fine then," Hubbard said. "We'll let this wagon train roll out in the morning, and while they disappear to the west, we'll watch for these three straggler wagons to come from the east. We won't need to be in any hurry to get out and get moving in the morning. I'd like to see with my own eyes that all of them get moving."

"I can agree to that," Winthrop said.

"And when the time comes, I want to get in close and do the work without firing a shot. Take no chance that Zeke's brother hears shots. I'm concerned enough that we might have stirred up a hornets nest at that Indian camp. I don't need some trail emigrants on our backtrail, too."

"Knives it is," Winthrop said.

One of the men, Hutson, came over with a biscuit broken in half and some charred bacon stuffed between the two pieces. He took a healthy bite and sat down on the rock beside Hubbard. He chewed for a long time, watching the people camped at the wagons.

"Think if I went down there I might find a woman who'd be willing to lay with me tonight?" Hutson asked.

Winthrop laughed.

"Doubtful. Them's all white women over there. You'd do better finding yourself an Indian camp with all the men gone from it."

Hutson grunted a reply.

"It's too bad for us they're so many and we're so few," he said. "We might find good property in some of them wagons."

"We may yet come across something worthwhile," Winthrop said. "Our honorable captain, Mr. Hubbard, has arranged for us to have a spot of good luck."

"Is that right?" Hutson asked through a mouthful of food.

"They've got some stragglers," Hubbard said. "Three wagons traveling behind the main body of the wagon train. Tomorrow, or maybe the next day, they're going to pass right by here, and we're going to get ourselves a wagon and increase our supplies."

23

—— ※ ——

"Don't look at me like that," Zeke Townes chided his dog.

The dog seemed to have an innate understanding that for weeks they'd been moving west and now they'd made an abrupt change in direction. They'd gone maybe six or eight miles back toward the east, Zeke's face burning in the afternoon sun as he rode along on his repaired saddle. He'd gathered up his belongings, scattered on the plain by the Indians who attacked him, loaded the pannier and put it on the bay. He'd saddled Duke and stepped into the stirrup, thinking of resuming his journey to Bridger's.

But he couldn't shake from his mind the thought that he should turn back.

Somewhere behind him, his wife, his son, and his brother's family were walking toward an outfit of hostile Indians. They'd spared his life, but maybe not on purpose. Maybe they thought one of those blows to the head had killed him. For all Zeke knew, these Indians might intend to kill every white person they encountered. Perhaps it was dumb luck and not mercy that left him alive.

So he wheeled Duke and called to Towser and started back with a quickened pace. The horses and dog were all revived with the presence of fresh water, and Zeke didn't bother to take it easy on them.

He kept Duke moving at a lope for as long as he could go. He didn't worry that he had no lead rope. The bay followed along. And if he stopped following, Zeke was willing to abandon the bay to get back to his family. Towser did his best to keep up, too, though twice he got distracted by prairie dogs or some varmint and chased off to the north. But each time, Towser reappeared.

Now, though, the dog had stopped and seemed unwilling to keep going.

"I know what I'm doing. You can come with me or not."

The look on the dog's face reflected Zeke's own thoughts. He'd set himself on an impossible mission.

Somehow, he would have to overtake those Indians who were hours ahead of him. From all appearances, they were moving light and fast. Not only would he have to overtake them, but if he was going to get ahead of the Indians and warn Elias and the others of the presence of Indians, he would also have to overtake them and avoid them, which seemed an impossibility.

And how could he ride back and warn the wagon train when he was banished from the wagon train? Banishment on the trail was no idle matter. If he returned, there would be some among them who would call for a hanging. Marcus Weiss, surely, would demand that he be hanged – or in the absence of a tree, shot dead. Elias would never do it, but if enough of the members of the wagon train demanded it, Elias might well find himself helpless to stop it.

The Indians, if they saw him a second time, would almost surely finish the job they'd left undone. And his former fellow travelers might well do it if the Indians did not.

Still, something had to be done. He couldn't know that his family was riding toward danger without giving them some sort of warning.

He had a vision of himself back at Bridger's Fort, waiting for a wagon train that would never turn up. He and others riding back to rescue them. Finding them all dead, their bodies mutilated by the vengeful Indians. Zeke living out his days knowing that he could have gone back and warned them and prevented it all. That vision would never come to pass. If he had to surrender his own life in an effort to save his family, then so be it.

"Come on, Towser," Zeke said, giving a tug to Duke's reins to point him back east. The dog watched as the gray horse and the bay started moving. He was panting pretty good. After a while, Zeke looked over his shoulder and saw the dog following them.

At dusk, Zeke dropped the pannier and its contents beside the wagon ruts on the trail, keeping only spare shot and powder. He switched the saddle from Duke to the bay horse. He took a drink from his canteen. Zeke picked Towser up and put him in the saddle, then mounted the bay. Once he got the bay facing east, Duke actually galloped a little ways ahead.

Zeke intended to keep moving through the night, hoping it would solve two of his problems. In the darkness, he hoped he could both overtake and slip past the Indians. The trick would be knowing they were there before they knew he was there. It could be that he would simply walk right past their camp, neither party aware of the other.

He rode the bay until the sun was completely down and then Zeke dismounted and put Towser on his own feet.

In the dark, he couldn't do more than keep the horses at a walk. The stars and moon provided enough light that he could keep an eye on both of them and be certain that neither wandered off. He led the bay for a while with the reins but then looped the reins over the saddle horn and just let the horses walk with him. When one or the other of them got distracted, he'd go over and give them a tug to keep them moving.

It was slow going, tedious at night with nothing to look at and no evidence beyond the soreness inside his boots to suggest that he was getting anywhere. One foot and then the other. One foot and then the other. How far did the Indians get before he started in pursuit? And if his instinct was correct that they were pursuing Hubbard and his outfit, would they also be traveling through the night?

The wind might have let up, but it didn't quit, and as the night wore on, it blew chilly. Zeke wished now he'd kept a blanket to throw over his shoulders. For some distance, he took up the reins and walked directly beside the bay, trying to get himself downwind where the horse might break the breeze some. That didn't hardly do any good, although he did think he felt a little warmer being up close to the animal.

Towser whined a little. The horses would be okay without sleep, but the dog ran hard through the day and needed sleep. Zeke picked him up and put him on the saddle and held a hand on the dog to keep him balanced there, but the effort was more than the value of it. Towser was good about staying in the saddle in Zeke's lap for stretches, but he wasn't much of a horseman on his own. After a while, Zeke decided the fight wasn't worth it, so he let the dog down.

He tried to imagine how far he'd gone and how far he might have to go to reach the wagon train.

He remembered hearing about a man back in Paducah who walked a hundred miles to Dyersburg, Tennessee in less than two days, spending some portion of a night walking. Zeke didn't think he had a hundred miles to go to get to the wagon train. He'd lost most of his concept of distance being out here on his own, but he figured he'd gone about a hundred and fifty miles since coming through the Devil's Gate. Surely by now Marie and the wagon train had cleared that obstacle.

While he wanted his own distance to be short, he feared that the Indians had such a jump on him that maybe they had already reached the wagon train. Maybe all his effort would prove futile and his fears of those Indians murdering his family had already come to pass.

At some point, Zeke got into the saddle with Towser again. He hugged the dog close to him for warmth, and Towser settled in and slept. Zeke dozed some, too, but he fought the urge to fall into a deep sleep.

His head throbbed from the bashing he'd taken, and he felt every bruise and cut them Indians had marked upon him. And in his mind, he pleaded for dawn to break the horizon.

He was surprised not to reach the Sweetwater again. He did not think he'd gone so far ahead of it, and now wondered how close he might have been to the Green River and, ultimately, Bridger's Fort, when he was attacked. A hundred miles? He thought so, but was not sure.

He also had to wonder if he'd reached his farthest point on his western journey and would never make it so far west again.

If the Indians did not get him and he found the wagon train, Marcus Weiss might well insist he be hanged for returning after banishment.

24

—— • ——

Overnight, Elias Townes couldn't sleep.

He'd doubled the night watch and told the men standing guard to be especially cautious of Hubbard and his outfit. Though they'd been congenial enough, through the last of the day and over supper and into the evening, Elias couldn't shake a feeling that there was something about those men he didn't care for.

"They're just men making their way on the trail, same as us," Madeline Townes told her husband.

"Maybe. But I'm worried for Zeke. Alone out there, encountering these men. I gave Zeke a lot of money."

"They don't know that," Madeline said.

"No, but they might be the sorts who would try to find out."

As the time neared for the family to leave Kentucky, Jason Winter asked Elias for permission to marry his eldest daughter, Maggie. Elias had made it clear: – the family intended to make the westward trek, and Maggie would be coming, too. That was fine, the young Winter said. He'd make his life in Oregon if he could make it there with Maggie Townes. Elias was none too thrilled with the idea. Maggie wasn't but sixteen-years-old, old enough for marriage, maybe, but younger still than Elias had envisioned. But Maggie made a fuss, saying she would stay with one of her uncles in Paducah if Elias refused Jason Winter. So there'd been a wedding, and Elias gave the bride and groom a wagon, and he brought an unexpected son-in-law along on the western migration.

Through the early morning hours, Jason Winter kept a rifle in his hand and his eyes on the strangers' camp at his father-in-law's request. When the sun broke, Elias went around the camp hurrying all of the emigrants, urging them to make fast with their breakfast and to hurry getting their teams hitched. It seemed that everyone had one problem or another – an uncooperative ox or a need to refill a water barrel, or a horse that had gone missing in the night.

When at last the wagons started to move, Jason Winter continued at his post, his rifle leaning against a large rock while he sat in the dirt and watched the distant camp. Jason's horse was saddled but not tied, just picking at some of the dry prairie grass. Elias went to him, mounted on Tuckee.

"Don't linger too long, Jace," Elias said.

"I'm coming straight away," Jason told his father-in-law. "What bothers me is, they ain't made the first move toward breaking camp and riding on. You'd think they'd be in a hurry to make the most of daylight."

Elias glanced over at the camp. The horses were all gathered in a rope corral. The men leisured around the remnants of a campfire.

"Well, it's not our business," Elias said. "I'll just be glad to put them behind us."

The last of the wagons was moving now, and the cow column had the livestock going right alongside them. In an hour, they'd be separated, the livestock beginning to fall behind the wagons some. They kicked up a tremendous dust, all those beasts milling in the dry grass.

Elias rubbed dirt from his eyes and then gave Tuckee's reins a pull, walking the horse up toward Hubbard's camp. He was better than halfway there when Hubbard came out a little ways to meet him. They made no effort to pack up and move. Campfires were still burning, coffee pots still steaming.

"Mr. Hubbard," Elias called. "I reckon we'll bid you a good journey now."

"And to you, too, Mr. Townes," Hubbard said back, holding up a hand to shield his eyes from the sun.

"I do appreciate you feeding my brother and bringing us news of him."

"Glad to do it," Hubbard said. "I reckon he's at Bridger's by now, butt in a rocker and feet propped on a table. He'll be waiting on you, I'm sure."

"I hope so. It was unfortunate business that sent him away from us, but I'm eager to be reunited."

"Ha!" Hubbard said. "I'll tell you, Mr. Townes, you're a better man than me. If I was leading a wagon train and they told me to banish my own kin, I'd tell them to try and make me. Hush up your complaints or go on about your own way."

"Maybe you're the better man," Elias said. The guilt of his brother's banishment never far from his mind.

Tuckee danced, and Elias tightened the reins and brought the horse back around to face Hubbard. As he did, he cast a look over Hubbard's men, sitting behind the man up among the big rocks where they'd camped. They looked like so many vultures, hungry and waiting.

"Safe travels back to Missouri," Elias said.

"Safe travels on to Oregon City," Hubbard said. "Is there a message you'd like us to give to the wagons behind you?"

The words struck Elias like a lead ball to the gut. He realized in that instant that even as the bulk of the Townes Party moved on and left Hubbard safely behind, the most vulnerable of them – the small band making their way alone – would be easy prey for ten hard men.

"Huh," Elias said, frowning. He needed to think what to do, but suddenly he found that his mind wasn't clear. Hubbard was looking at him, a curious frown on his face. The other men were watching him, too. Elias mumbled something – farewell or good-bye, he didn't know what – and turned Tuckee toward his son-in-law who was just now mounting his horse. He galloped the distance, and Jason, seeing him coming, waited in the saddle.

"Marie and Gabriel behind us," Elias said, the words spluttered from his mouth. "Ride back and warn them. Tell them about this party of men. And then stay back with them, Jace. Help protect them if necessary."

Jason Winter stared astonished at his father-in-law. He was just a boy, still. Hardly older than Gabe, and less experienced in hunting and hard work. Jason came from a family of merchants. He was ill suited for this request, but he was all Elias had presently.

"There's no time to spare," Elias said. "If I ride ahead and ask Henry Blair or one of the Tucker brothers to do it, these men might intercept them and stop them from delivering the warning. You must ride now, while the wagon train is still here in full view and Hubbard and his men cannot give chase without being seen. You have a fresh horse, a rifle in hand, and a canteen. You go now, at a good lope. You don't stop or look back or delay yourself in any way whatsoever. And when you get there, you stand by with the wagons. Help protect them. And if you encounter these men, you do not allow them to approach at all. Tell Caleb Driscoll. Tell Mr. Pilcher. These men can't come near the wagons."

Jason Winter nodded his head, but continued to appear wide-eyed, as if his father-in-law had slapped him across the face.

The two men sat their horses face to face, looking at each other. Elias nodded his head to prompt the boy.

"You've got to go, Jace. You've got to ride now."

Jason Winter nodded back.

"Tell Maggie –"

"I'll tell her," Elias said. "Just go."

Elias watched as Jason Winter rode back to the east to rendezvous with Gabe and Pilcher and Marie.

"That damn Marcus Weiss will be useless in a fight," Elias said to Tuckee. "But they've got Jerry Bennett back with them, and Jerry's a hand. Caleb, too. I reckon Jeff Pilcher can fight. Gabe's a marksman, and Jason – he can pull a trigger and load a rifle. But it's still damn poor odds."

Elias glanced at the camp of men up among the rocks. If they'd noticed Jason riding back, or cared, there was no indication from the camp. The men were up and moving around, mostly. It looked like they were packing up, getting ready to leave. Not that there was much to pack.

"Five good men against ten," Elias said to himself, and three names came to mind. Henry Blair and the Tucker brothers, Johnny and Billy. Those three, and himself, they could ride back and make the odds better than even. The Tucker brothers were worth five men in a fight, and Henry Blair had proved himself capable. But could he risk the main body of the wagon train? What lives would be left in jeopardy – what jeopardy might they face? If this trail had taught anything to him it was this: Disaster could lurk at the next hill or hollow, the next bend in the river, whatever was just beyond the horizon. Elias knew it would be damned irresponsible to strip the Tucker brothers from the cow column and pull both himself and Henry Blair away from the wagons.

To the west, the wagons were rolling and the cows were kicking up dust. To the east, Jason Winter was riding at a gallop, and even as Elias watched, he rode down into a hollow and disappeared from sight. Above him, a couple hundred yards away, Hubbard and his men remained at their camp. They'd seen Jace ride off. There could be no doubt about that. Perhaps Elias was mistaken about his misgivings. Hubbard had been nothing but friendly. And if those men had offered any violence to Zeke, they didn't steal either of the horses Zeke had taken. Elias had looked over their horses, and neither Duke nor the bay were among them.

At length, satisfied that his son-in-law had enough of a jump that Hubbard and his men would never catch up to him, Elias gave a tug on Tuckee's reins and turned the horse west.

"All I've done since they elected me captain of this train has been done for the common good," Elias said to the horse. "I can't abandon all that now. I've a job to do, to see this train to Bridger's Fort with the most of them arriving safely. I can't strip away the best men out of my own fears."

He didn't hurry, though, and he kept a watch over his shoulder on Hubbard and his men.

They made no move to abandon their camp. They did not send riders to try to intercept Jason. They showed no outward sign of hostility at all.

By the time Elias reached the wagon train, the wagons had moved away from the cow column. So it was that he rode into the cloud of dust first, and caught up to Johnny Tucker riding on the northern flank of the livestock. Johnny had his bandanna covering nose and mouth, and already a thin layer of dust caked to his face around his eyes.

"Morning, Johnny," Elias said.

"Morning, Mr. Townes."

"All's well?"

"Everything's good, sir."

"I don't think they'll offer us any trouble, but you keep your eyes open on our backtrail, Johnny. You watch for those men who camped alongside us last night. If you see them coming, you'd better give a shout."

"I'll do it, Mr. Townes."

The hands all looked to Zeke as a friend. He was about the same age as the rest of them, he rolled up his sleeves when they rolled up their sleeves, he worked harder than the hardest working among them. He had their respect, but he also had their friendship. Elias, being older and always having been the boss, he wasn't the friend of the men. He had their respect, and he worked every bit as hard as Zeke. But he never had their friendship.

He passed by the Page brothers, up at the front of the column, and gave his hat a wave to them without stopping for conversation.

It being morning, most of the children and women were out walking alongside the wagons. They walked in the morning before the heat of the day got to them. Then they alternated women and children in the wagons. One or two of the women had taken to riding horses. Most of the men walked beside their oxen, whip in hand, to drive the wagons. Those who had hired drivers rode horses, if they had them, or walked with their wives.

Elias chatted here and there with the emigrants as he made his way up the wagon train. Just a friendly word of greeting or a small joke.

"We're almost to Oregon," he called out to Wiser McKinney. "Just a few thousand more miles."

"We'll be there any day," McKinney called back.

Up ahead now, Elias could see his wife and children.

His oldest daughter Maggie – Maggie Winter, now – drove her wagon in the absence of her husband. He would have to stop and talk to her, tell her where Jason had got off to, and why. His middle son, Christian, drove one of the family's two wagons while Madeline drove the other. The second wagon contained nothing but tools, supplies necessary to begin business in Oregon. The first wagon, in the capable hands of Elias's wife, that held the family's valuables and those things they would need to begin a life in this faraway land.

As he drew even with Maggie, Elias swung himself from the saddle and went on foot, keeping Tuckee's reins in hand.

"I've sent Jason back to your Aunt Marie," Elias said.

Maggie furrowed her brow.

"For what reason?"

"I sent him to deliver a message that they should be wary of those men who camped beside us last night."

The furrows in her brow grew deeper still.

"Do you think there's danger?" Maggie asked.

"I think we should avoid danger if we can," Elias said. "And that's why I sent him back. So that your brother and the others will be aware of these men and not allow them to get too close."

"Is he coming back?"

"Not immediately, no. I asked him to stay with them – one more man to help protect them."

Maggie took a sharp breath.

"Should we not stop the wagons and wait for them to catch up to us?"

Elias let out a heavy breath.

"We cannot do that, Maggie. I'm sorry. But we're farther behind schedule than we should be. At all costs we must avoid getting caught by the snow when we get into the Blue Mountains of Oregon Territory. Every stop we make, every day we lose, brings us one day closer to disaster. We'll lose a day repairing Zeke's wagon at the fort, and who knows how long it takes to rest and resupply there. Two days? Three? We've got to push onward."

Maggie looked as if her heart was breaking.

"There's nothing to fear," Elias said. "Jason will be fine."

Elias stepped back into the saddle and started to ride forward, intending to have a similar conversation with his wife now. But far out ahead, he saw a rider sitting on his horse, alone and not moving. Elias loped up toward Madeline and called to her.

"Is that Henry up ahead?"

"It is."

Henry Blair, stopped on a rise ahead of them, maybe a half mile or more.

"I'd better go see what's wrong."

25

With Elias holding back, Henry Blair took the initiative to ride ahead of the wagon train as it got started that morning.

On a typical day, Elias rode out front and Henry Blair would stay back near the cow column, keeping an eye on the last of the wagons to make sure no one fell out of the line or experienced any trouble. From the back, he could watch all the wagons for a problem.

He'd advanced maybe three quarters of a mile ahead of the front wagon and then kept roughly to the train's pace. He was looking for anything – coyotes, a prairie dog village that might cause problems, a swamped swale that they needed to ride around – though he'd seen nothing like that in the longest time since they'd come into this dry country. But the biggest thing he watched for was marauders, whether they be Indians looking to steal some cattle or a gang of outlaws terrorizing emigrants.

Henry knew better than any of the others about the potential to run into rough men. He'd been out here before, as far as Bridger's, anyway, and he'd seen the sorts of men who rode this trail. Men like those freighters who'd camped beside them the night before. It was Henry's opinion that Elias was right to double the night watch and be wary of those men.

They'd been maybe an hour moving on the trail, Henry riding out front, when he caught sight of something in the distance. He was up on top of a rise and had the best vantage he'd have for some time, so Henry reined up and waited. He sat there for several minutes without seeing what he'd seen again, and then he heard a horse approaching from behind. He turned to see Elias Townes.

"Hello, Henry. Everything all right?"

"I don't know, Mr. Townes," Henry said. "I seen something up yonder."

Elias was up even with him now, and pulled reins to stop the palomino.

"What do you think you saw?"

"Maybe a coyote," Henry said.

"An animal, then?"

"Surely an animal. But I'll say it could have been a dog."

"A dog?" Elias said.

There were a couple dozen dogs in the wagon train. Some of them working dogs that helped with the livestock. Some offered protection – they'd bark and raise a fuss if Indians approached at night or if there was a snake in the trail. Zeke kept a whole host of dogs, and always preferred having a dog around. Elias looked back now and could see some of the dogs walking along with the train. Two of them were off chasing each other a little ways from the wagon train.

"Not one of ours, is it?"

"I didn't see none run ahead of us this morning," Henry said. "Though I suppose one might have."

"Which way was it bound?" Elias asked.

"Coming toward us," Henry said.

Elias was looking at Henry in that moment and didn't have his eyes ahead when Henry said, "Oh, hell! Mr. Townes, look there!"

Now he turned and looked ahead, and indeed there was some shadow far along the trail.

"That a man, mounted, Mr. Townes," Henry said.

Elias looked, squinting his eyes at the distant horizon. As far out as he could see. He thought Henry was probably right, a man on a horse.

"Indians?" Elias said.

"I'd reckon it could be. Should I halt the wagon train?"

"Always the pressure to keep rolling. Always the reasons to stop."

"Yes, sir. It ain't a trail for the meek."

"No, Henry. Ride back. Tell Captain Walker to ready for trouble. Get the men armed, but don't stop them from moving. You and some of the others ready yourselves for a fight."

"And you, sir?"

"I'm going to ride ahead a ways and see what this is."

Elias felt a queasy disturbance in his gut. Their recent trouble with the Indians' attempt to steal cattle had him leery to encounter Indians again anytime soon. He didn't like it, either, that there was a lone Indian ahead of them. One lone Indian out on the prairie probably meant two dozen he couldn't see.

A dog and a man?

It couldn't be Zeke. He'd know better. Zeke would never put him in the position of having to make a decision like that.

A man banished from a wagon train who came back, he was a man tempting worse, a man seeking harsher judgment. Banishment on this trail might well mean death, and everyone knew it. The banished and the judges alike knew that. Even if he was starved and dying, Zeke couldn't come back. And he wouldn't. Never would his brother put Elias in the position of having to condemn Zeke to death.

Still, as he rode on forward, Elias could see two horses now, and one man. And Henry had seen a dog, somewhere.

And now Elias heard the dog, an angry bark, and he came running up out of a nearby hollow, his appearance so sudden and the bark so vicious that Tuckee, dipped his head and spun like he was going to wheel and run.

"Whoa!" Elias shouted, and he pulled hard on the reins, lifting the horse's head and dragging him back around. "Hey, easy there!"

Only now, with the horse under control, did Elias get a good look at the dog racing toward him. Black and white fur all a blur as he charged forward, and then the angry barks turned to high pitched squeals. The dog recognized Elias just as Elias recognized Towser.

"Damn," Elias muttered under his breath. If this was Towser, there could be no doubt of the identity of the rider out on the horizon.

Elias got the horse fully under control and then dropped down from the saddle to meet Towser as he came at a run. The dog barked all around Elias's feet, spinning circles, and Elias had trouble getting hands on the dog to get him under control.

"What are you doing here, boy?" Elias said, patting the dog as Towser finally calmed down and leaned against Elias's legs. "What's Zeke doing here?"

Elias straightened up and looked off to the west. Zeke was still maybe a mile out, but Elias could see him clear enough now. Two horses and a man. But he couldn't see the pannier on the spare horse, and Elias wondered if Zeke had run into trouble, lost his supplies, and maybe risked returning to the wagon train for sustenance. The dog looked plenty well fed, but that didn't surprise Elias. Zeke was the type who would suffer to spare his dog.

"All right, Towser. Go get Zeke," Elias said. He gave a tug to the cinch and then climbed back onto Tuckee's back. Maybe he could meet Zeke far enough out, get him turned around now before it became an issue. Marcus Weiss wasn't with the wagon train and wouldn't know of Zeke's return. That might be the one thing that saved his brother. But Elias had nothing in his possession – no morsel of food that he could give to Zeke.

They met down in the hollow from which Towser had appeared.

The first thing Elias noticed as they neared each other was that Zeke had lost his hat. Then he realized that the bay wasn't on a lead rope. But as they grew nearer, Elias saw the rest of it.

"What's happened to you, brother?" Elias said. Zeke's face was caked with blood. One eye badly swollen. Those parts of his face not black and blue were red from the sun.

"Attacked by Indians," Zeke said.

Both men halted their horses facing each other. They did not embrace as brothers might, nor were there smiles of greeting.

"Lord have mercy," Elias said, confounded by his brother's appearance. "How badly are you hurt?"

"Not so bad," Zeke said. "It looks worse than it is, I'm sure."

"It looks bad enough," Elias said. He noticed the two rifles and the two saddle guns.

"They left you armed and alive?"

"I don't know that they left me alive on purpose, but they only stole a couple of things."

"You're blessed more than most," Elias said. "But why have you come back, Ezekiel? Surely, you know the consequences."

Zeke ignored the question.

"Have you seen the Indians? Maybe fifteen or twenty of them, I never did count."

"We've seen no Indians for days," Elias said. "We had a band try to ride off with some of our cattle, but that was days ago."

"No," Zeke said. "These would have passed you in the last day or two."

"We've not seen them," Elias said.

Zeke looked back over his shoulder, as if he expected them to appear there.

"Maybe I passed them during the night," Zeke said. His exhaustion fully evident to his brother.

"Have you ridden through the night?"

"I have," Zeke said, but Elias understood that Zeke had other priorities.

"Just to warn us of Indians?"

Zeke seemed distracted, looking over his shoulder again.

"Listen, Elias. I encountered some men some days ago. Hubbard and some others."

"I know about them," Elias said. "They camped beside us last night."

"And they've moved on?" Zeke said. "They're going east behind you?"

"They are," Elias said. "They told me you'd camped with them."

"They're scalphunters, Elias. They killed women and children at a camp in the Wind Mountains." Elias looked to the north, but down in the hollow he could not see the peaks of the distant Winds. "Did they show you the scalps?"

Elias shook his head.

"They didn't," he said. And because his brother seemed so bothered, he added, "I'm sorry, Zeke. I never saw them."

"So many of them, drying on a pole."

Elias began to wonder if his brother had not been driven insane by the rough treatment he'd received. He had bad wounds on his head. Perhaps he'd been knocked senseless. It happened sometimes to men who got kicked in the head by a mule or a horse.

"The Indians," Zeke said. "I think they must be the men from that summer camp. I think they must be pursuing those scalphunters. I don't know what they might do to a wagon train if they come across it."

"Have you eaten?" Elias asked. Other than the visible injuries, Zeke looked all right. He didn't look gaunt or like he lacked for water. Maybe a little thin, but not wasting. But he seemed so unhinged, and the things he said absurd. Elias got the drift of it – Hubbard and his men had committed a massacre at the Indian camp, and there were Indians on the warpath. But these things were no concern for a wagon train. They were too well armed. No small band of Indians would be foolish enough as to attack a full wagon train. And if they did, there were plenty enough fit men here who could fight.

"I've eaten," Zeke said. "I'm fit enough."

"You can't be here, Zeke," Elias said, and now he heard the plea in his own voice. "You've got to go. Now, before the others see you. Ride back the other direction a ways and wait for me by the river. I'm going to go back to the wagon train, tell them everything is fine. You've lost your pack. I'll get you some supplies. And I can see about dressing that wound on your head. Clean you up a bit so you're presentable riding into Bridger's."

Zeke took a breath. Steadied himself. Elias watched him closely.

"Hubbard and his men are gone?" Zeke said. "You're sure of it?"

"We left them back a ways. I've told the boys to keep a watch on the backtrail, but I don't think they're going to follow us."

"Those Indians are after them, Elias. I worry what they'll do when they see you."

"But you didn't encounter them again?" Elias asked. "They attacked you, and they rode east?"

"That's right."

"And you rode east, but you didn't encounter them. And we've not seen them. Zeke, I think they've probably gone on some different way. Maybe back up into the Winds."

Zeke shook his head.

"I must have passed them in the night," he said. "I'm telling you, Elias, I saw those men, the rage in their faces. They'll not quit until they've had blood."

"But if it's Hubbard they're after, they'll not molest us."

"You don't know that," Zeke said.

"We're a full wagon train," Elias said. "We've got a score of armed men, and rifles enough to outfit an army. Even if they are bold enough to make an attack on us, it will be a short-lived affair."

Zeke seemed to calm a mite. He took a breath and let it out.

"You need some sleep, brother. But more than that, you need to move on ahead of us before folks see you and get some ideas. Now do as I say. Take Towser, take the horses, go on back the way you come. Go a couple of miles. Three miles, maybe. Wait for me by the river. I'll go back to the train and get you some supplies that will last you. I'll tell them it was an Indian me and Henry seen, and I'm buying him off with some flour and bacon. I'd clean you up, dress that wound, and then you ride on. Do you need a fresh horse?"

"The horses are fine," Zeke said.

Elias felt great relief that his brother was agreeable now, that he'd calmed down from the fit he'd been having. Was it so much time alone on the trail? Was it the bashing to the head?

"Bring Marie with you," Zeke said.

"I can't do that, Zeke," Elias said.

"Find some excuse to make to the others. I need to see her, need to see that she's well and whole."

"No, Zeke. You're not understanding. Marie's wagon had an accident. Broken axle. We couldn't repair it, so we put it on skids. She's a day's ride behind us."

"Alone?" Zeke asked, and his eyes suddenly looked crazy again.

"Not alone. Pilcher and Marcus Weiss are with her. Jerry Bennett, Caleb, Gabe."

"And she's not yet passed Hubbard and his outfit?"

"No, but I sent Jace Winter back to have them watch for Hubbard. I didn't much care –"

But whatever Elias was going to say he didn't care for was lost in the moment. Zeke gave Duke a slap on the rump with the ends of his reins and called out, "Ha!"

The horse broke into a gallop, going like he'd been in a corral for the last month. The bay jumped to it, too, having followed the gray horse for so many days, it didn't seem to know how to do anything different. And they were headed east, of course, bounding up the hollow and toward the approaching wagon train.

"Damnation," Elias said, and Towser broke into a run, barking as he chased down Zeke and the two horses.

At least he had sense enough to give the wagon train a wide berth.

Henry Blair had gotten a half dozen men together in a battle line ahead of the wagons, but their guns stood silent as Zeke cut out across the prairie, maybe as much as a mile and a half north of the wagons but within about half a mile of the northern flank of the livestock.

Elias rode back toward the wagons, not certain of what was best to do.

As he approached the train, Reverend Marsh called out, "Mr. Townes? Was that your brother who just passed us by?"

"It was, Reverend Marsh," Elias said, seeing no need to lie.

"He knows returning to the wagon train after banishment is a crime punishable by death?" Reverend Marsh said.

The preacher was there with Captain Walker, both William and Cody Page, Noah Bloom, and Henry Blair. Each of the men had a horse and a rifle, ready to fend off Indians if that's what Henry had seen.

"As you can see, Reverend, my brother did not return to the wagon train."

"Well, where's he going?" Cody Page asked.

"He's been attacked," Elias said.

"By that man, Hubbard?" Henry Blair asked.

"No, Henry. He said a band of Indians attacked him, and he warned that they might still be ahead of us somewhere. We'll need to ride guards ahead of the wagon train, and all the men should be armed and ready should we fall under attack."

Elias looked east, beyond the wagon train. The cow column had kicked up dust that seemed to go from here to Missouri, and through the dust and the approaching wagons, Elias had lost sight entirely of his brother.

"But where is he bound now?" Reverend Marsh asked. "Surely, he has not decided to go back?"

"I believe he's concerned about his wife's safety," Elias said. "And perhaps he's right to be. I took a bad feeling from that man Hubbard, and I have my own concerns that they'll see those three wagons behind us as easy prey. I'm thinking of taking some men and following behind him."

"You cannot do that," Reverend Marsh said. "We're already less protected than we should be. There's Indians ahead, and you're talking about dividing our numbers even more. Weakening the defenses of the wagon train? I heavily object, Mr. Townes."

It wasn't a plea from the preacher, but a logical argument in favor of protecting the main body of the wagon train. And Elias knew the sound wisdom in what the preacher said. Zeke had been beaten something awful by those Indians. He was lucky to have his hair. And he was right to think the wagons might be a target for a band of enraged Indians. And every soul in the Townes Party knew the same thing that every soul who traveled this trail knew – it was damned risky business. Lives were lost by the scores every season. Illness, accident, disaster – and murder. Everybody who set off west from the Missouri River took their chance, and everybody knew that their primary responsibility had to be to protect the common good of the wagon train. If separated from the wagon train, an emigrant simply had to do their own best to survive.

"I'll go," Henry Blair said.

"I'll ride along, too," Cody Page said.

169

"Mr. Townes! You can't allow it," Reverend Marsh objected.

Elias exhaled a heavy breath.

"We'll stay with the wagons," he said. "Henry, you and Mr. Bloom ride out to the north. Stay within sight, but take up a position north, and in advance of the wagon trains. Keep your eyes open and signal back if you should see anything. Cody and William, Captain Walker, you'll ride with me here at the front. Reverend Marsh, if you'd be so good as to ride back and let all the men know to keep their arms nearby. Tell them we fear danger from Indians."

"I'll do it," Reverend Marsh said. "And, Mr. Townes, I'll not mention to anyone that your brother has returned to the wagon train. Some dispensation should be given when we consider that he rode back to warn us of danger."

Elias shot a look at Captain Walker, who equally bore a look of disgust at the preacher's words. In that moment, more so than ever before, Elias deeply regretting including Reverend Marsh in his brother's tribunal.

The men riding protection spread out as Elias had instructed, covering a distance about the width of two miles from the river bank.

They soon came upon a river crossing, their third crossing of the Sweetwater in the last week.

They rode not much more than half an hour when Henry Blair began to wave his hat as a signal to Elias Townes, and Elias brought Tuckee up to a lope. He kept his eyes on the horizon as he rode out to Henry and Noah, but he saw nothing that would raise an alarm.

"What is it, Henry?"

"Mr. Townes, I thought you would want to know, we're coming up now to the South Pass. You'll not reckon it, but this is the highest point of the whole trail."

"We've not even climbed," Elias said, looking back at the flat expanse.

"This is it, all the same, Mr. Townes. We're more than seven thousand feet here. It's the backbone of the Rockies."

"The Continental Divide," Elias said. He'd been annoyed at first, but it occurred to him now he'd likely never be here again, and he was glad to commemorate the moment, if only by knowing of it. He'd ride back and pass the word to the others in the wagon train. "All the water from here flows west."

"Yes, sir," Henry said. "And this is the spot. I recollect when I came through here before. It's that hill, yonder. The one pointed on top."

"A hundred and thirty miles to Fort Bridger, then?" Elias said.

"About that. Yes, sir," Henry said.

"Then we should do well to keep the wagons moving."

Elias rode back down to the wagon train, and he shared the news with the others that they were now moving through South Pass. Most of the other travelers seemed unimpressed. They wanted their landmarks to smack of the impressive – Chimney Rock and Scotts Bluff, Devil's Gate or even Independence Rock. Here, there was nothing to see, no impressive prominence.

But as he returned to his spot at the front of the wagon train, Elias saw something on a hill far to the north of the wagon train. He did not doubt what it was. Mounted men, fifteen or twenty of them. Sitting their ponies and watching the wagon train pass.

Henry Blair and Noah Bloom were riding back to him now, and Elias stopped Tuckee and sat, waiting on them. He watched the Indians who watched him.

"You see them, Mr. Townes?" Henry asked, coming at the gallop.

"I see them, Henry. They've shown no aggression. They seem intent to let us pass."

"Should we ride back to protect the flank of the cow column?" Henry asked. It was as much suggestion as it was a question.

"Get Cody Page and ride back to cover the livestock," Elias said. "But I do not think these men intend to steal our cattle."

"No, sir. I don't think so, neither," Henry said. "They wouldn't have showed themselves if they did."

"But God help my brother and the others behind us," Elias said, his thoughts on his oldest son. He regretted now sending back Jason Winter. If Maggie lost a husband and brother today, she would be inconsolable.

26

Johnny Hubbard did not care for Winthrop's plan, but the others in the company preferred it.

Wait and let the stragglers come to us, Winthrop suggested.

Hubbard couldn't deny one aspect of the plan. Just a few miles down the trail, the wagons would reach the final crossing of the Sweetwater River. Though this was probably the easiest river crossing of the trail, the wagons would still have to slow, take the crossing one at a time and at a cautious pace. There, they would be easy marks.

"They'll probably put the wagon riding on skids through first," Winthrop said. "That will slow the other two down even more. If we time our attack for while the middle wagon is in the water, we can catch them at their most vulnerable. I can take a couple of the boys across the river now and lay in wait for them on that side. When they're slow and distracted, we can strike. You come in from this side of the river, I'll come in from the other side."

Hubbard had wanted to get in close to the emigrants, keep the thing silent. But they'd seen that rider go back, and Hubbard agreed with Winthrop that the man's purpose was to warn the stragglers. "They probably won't let us get close, now," Hubbard had said.

So they'd thought about another plan. A way to get at them when they were virtually helpless. And the Sweetwater crossing was a good place to stage an ambush because they'd likely make camp once they got across the river.

"What if they arrive late in the day and make camp on this side of the river?" Hubbard said.

"It makes no difference," Winthrop said. "We can ford the river at the crossing without any trouble and still get at them easy enough."

Hubbard accepted that. He accepted all of it. Besides, it kept Winthrop happy and kept Hubbard in charge of the outfit. They'd get a wagon, which would make for a more comfortable crossing back to Missouri. They'd have blankets and extra supplies. Maybe they'd get some steers from the cow column – assuming these stragglers even had much in the way of livestock with them. Steers would mean a supply of beef. Maybe when they got down to the Platte they would stop long enough to butcher a cow and smoke some meat.

What worried Hubbard was those Indians behind them.

At some point, the men from the camp were going to return home. They were going to find their people murdered. They were going to go on the warpath, looking for revenge.

If it hadn't already happened, it would happen soon.

Hubbard didn't want to be in the South Pass when those Indians came looking for him. He didn't want to be at Independence Rock. He wanted to be beyond Fort Laramie. The Shoshone probably wouldn't chase that far. Hubbard thought of Fort Laramie as safety. It was a place to run to. There were soldiers there, and this time of year, some of them would be out patrolling the prairie. If they were attacked, any bit of good fortune could come to them near Fort Laramie. But probably more to the point, if there were Indians in pursuit of them, they'd not likely go beyond the fort down into the Platte valley.

Now, the question was how far back to the east were these stragglers. Would Hubbard and his men have to wait a day or two days? Would it be even more? And were they just sitting here waiting and giving those Indians on their back trail more time to catch up to them?

"Maybe some of these immigrants will be black haired," Winthrop said. "We can add to our scalps."

Another man in the group, Donny Haygood, piped in.

"If they's blondes, we can just sell them scalps back in Missouri and tell folks we come across a tribe of towheaded Injuns."

27

— · —

Z<small>EKE</small> T<small>OWNES</small> <small>SPOKE QUIETLY</small> to Towser.

"Keep it down, now," he said. "You be a good boy and don't go barking your head off."

He'd dropped down out of the saddle and picked up the dog and put him up on the saddle. Now he walked beside Duke, holding Towser in place. The bay stayed right with them.

Had it been later in the day, or if there was anything else out here to burn except twisted sagebrush and juniper from down by the riverbanks, Zeke would have ridden directly into Hubbard and his men. But the mid-morning sun ahead of him caught the thin trail of gray smoke rising up from a campfire ahead. The wind blew scattered the smoke almost at ground level, but it being sagebrush, it was dark enough for Zeke to see. He realized it must be Hubbard. So he veered off the trail, going wide to the north and using a small rise to shield himself from view.

The sun in his face hit against his pink and raw skin, and he could feel how burned his face was. Everything was misery, now. His feet ached from marching all through the night. His muscles were sore from the walking, and from the beating he'd taken. His head pounded. His face burned. To say nothing of the exhaustion that had grasped hold to him. Perhaps the worst ache he felt was that which came from behind his eyes – that ache for sleep. But he had to push on.

He kept his eye on that smoke, now off his right shoulder, and when he felt comfortable enough to approach, he brought Towser down to the ground, gripped the length of twine the dog wore as a collar, and walked up the incline of the rise, bent over to keep a hole on Towser. His worst fear was that the dog would start to bark and give him away. So he held the twine tight, crouched his way up the rise, and when he reached the precipice, he dropped down to the ground on his belly.

He'd come a mile or so north of Hubbard's camp, and though the men were camped in among a large outcropping of rock, Zeke could see them well enough. Ten men, a couple of campfires going. Just lounging around, making no effort to break camp and get on the move. Odd behavior for men trying to make it back to Missouri eight hundred miles away.

Towser sniffed at the air, smelling the smoke, and thought it was supper time. But Zeke held fast to the twine.

"All right, boy. You keep quiet."

He'd put eyes on them, which is what he wanted. He just needed to know for sure that it was Hubbard and his men.

Now Zeke returned down the hillside the same way he'd come up it, crouched and holding Towser's collar.

The dog whined a bit, wanting to go off and investigate the smells. But Zeke returned him to the saddle and kept going.

He had to wonder if he'd been wrong about the Indians. Maybe they weren't pursuing Hubbard and those other men at all. And maybe he was also wrong about Hubbard.

Zeke's head ached. His body ached. He wasn't thinking clearly. Everything felt like some sort of dream, like a nightmare that only got worse the deeper he got into it. Maybe all his thoughts were corrupted from the knock to the head.

He didn't know how far he would have to go to find Marie and Daniel. He didn't know if he would be traveling a day or two days. If they were delayed by even the smallest of matters, it might be three days. He knew he needed to rest and preserve his strength. If his fears were not unfounded – if the danger was real – he would be no use to them if he did not get some sleep.

The sun and traveler moved in opposite directions, and they soon caught each other. Zeke would have given everything he'd ever owned for a shade tree. His scalp burned. His nose burned. The tops of his ears were so painful that it shot stings of pain through him when he brushed back his long hair to tuck it behind his ears.

He was mounted again by now. Towser on foot. He'd worked his way back down to the trail, which brought him nearer the Sweetwater River. Towser came up from the bank at one point absolutely soaking wet, and Zeke felt a little jealous.

Hours later, ahead of him, Zeke could see some new thing. A darkness coming at him. The sun was setting and dusk was approaching from the east.

Marie and her little band would be stopped now.

It was time for Zeke to stop as well.

He bedded down by the trail, desperately wishing he had something to eat. He'd have taken a blanket, too, but the hunger was more present than the cold. Towser slept in a ball beside him and provided at least some warmth.

The hunger woke him.

Zeke opened his eyes and sighed heavily. Up in the night sky he could see the blue of early dawn. He sighed heavily as everything came back to him. If anything, sleeping on the ground had added to his aches and pains. Towser pawed at him when he sighed. There was no less comfort in getting up and moving around, so he did not linger there on the ground. He had no coffee to boil and no pot to boil it in, so a fire was pointless. It might warm him, but he'd be warm enough when the day came.

He tried to think of the last time he ate. Antelope steak. How many days ago? He did not know. He'd lost all track of time.

The blue light in the sky became a gray light all around, and he caught the two horses and brought them together. He saddled Duke again today. He put the pannier's straps on the bay. The canvas bags, of course, he'd abandoned so many miles back. He tucked his spare rifle and saddle gun – the weapons Elias had given him – into the straps. He put his rifle into the straps on his saddle and hung the holster of the saddle gun onto the saddle horn.

If his fears were confirmed and it was to be a fight – either with Hubbard or with those Indians – he'd come prepared.

Then they started to move again.

The animals were visibly weary, now. Towser and the two horses. They moved slower. Zeke's suspicion was that the dog had supplemented his last good meal with a prairie dog or two, but none of them had eaten well in a long time. The horses needed the oats that would be available at Bridger's Fort as much as Zeke needed a steak and some vegetables. He was thinking now as much about food as he was thinking of seeing Marie again. But he was also thinking about Marcus Weiss. The man would demand his head if he returned to the wagon train, even the part of the wagon train that had fallen behind.

He'd been in the saddle for a mile when a yellow light topped the distant horizon, and there was his friend the sun, come to torture his already burned face a little more.

Zeke cursed those Indians under his breath.

Another mile, and another, and then he saw something out on the horizon. They'd made an early start of it, probably setting out at first light. Three wagons and some spare oxen, moving toward him on the trail.

Zeke's heart leapt. For a moment, the hunger and the aches and the sunburn and the pounding in his head were all forgotten as the sight of Marie – not Marie, but the wagon, anyway – restored him. In that moment, Zeke felt as if he could fight off a hundred Indians and a hundred Hubbards. He would do whatever he had to do to protect his wife and son.

And in feeling restored, he also thought clearly.

"Ha!" he called to Duke, wheeling the horse to the north.

He did not have to risk his life by joining the wagons. He just had to be there to save them at the last moment.

28

—·—

CALEB DRISCOLL WAS WALKING beside the Weiss wagon, at the lead of the small column. The Weiss's children, three young children, were all in the wagon where they spent most of their time.

Caleb turned around and called back to Marie, next in line.

"I can't credit it, but there's a dog coming toward us," he said.

"A dog?" Marie Townes asked. "You're joking, Mr. Driscoll."

"No, ma'am. I ain't. It's a dog, sure enough."

Marie Townes moved out away from the wagon some where she could better see beyond her nephew who drove her wagon and Caleb Driscoll up in front, and her heart gave a start. It was indeed a dog, and he looked so much like Towser that her first thought was that her husband must be coming back. That black and white dog followed Zeke everywhere he went.

But her next thought was of Marcus Weiss. She could just see the man walking on the far side of his wagon. He walked behind his wife, and when she saw them like that, Marie had the impression of a dark spirit hovering over poor Mrs. Weiss.

Jason Winter, mounted and riding over near Jerry Bennett and the spare oxen, gave his horse a touch with his knee and rode out in front of the small group. Jason had delivered his message of warning, meeting up with the wagons the previous day, and then stayed on to provide one more man for protection.

But as Jason rode forward, one of the dogs traveling with the wagons broke off at a run. Marie thought the dog was going to fight the newcomer, what with the way he barked and carried on, but then she realized that it was Mustard, and Mustard and Towser were the best of friends. They came from different litters, of course, Mustard being a yellow dog. But they were about the same age and had always been together. Both of them followed Zeke to work every day back in Kentucky, and had since they were puppies. Marie was surprised that Zeke did not take them both when he was banished, but she knew that Zeke rated Mustard as a good protector and she believed he'd left him on purpose for that reason.

And now the two dogs began to run around, barking at each other, and chasing.

"It's Towser," Marie said.

"Ma'am?" Caleb asked.

"It's Towser," Marie said again, more loudly.

"Is that your husband's mutt?" Marcus Weiss demanded, turning on her and coming toward her. "If your husband has returned to this wagon train, I'll shoot him myself!"

"B'God you will!" Jerry Bennett barked. "You try it, Mr. Weiss, and I'll put you down quicker'n a lame horse."

Weiss recoiled, and Marie Townes smiled. Jerry Bennett was one of the men who worked for Elias and Zeke. He seldom spoke, even around the campfire at night. When she tried to make conversation with him, he had little to say, either about himself or anything else. But now he spoke with a calm authority that frightened Marcus Weiss into silence.

Towser ran to Marie and Daniel now, and the boy laughed and petted him as Towser bowled him over and licked him in the face, doing his happy squealing bark. But the smile quickly faded from Marie's face.

"Caleb? Do you see anything of Mr. Townes?" she asked.

Caleb had set his whip in Weiss's wagon and climbed up on the side of it, standing up tall and straining his neck for the best possible vantage.

"I don't, ma'am."

"Oh, Towser. What can it mean that you're here and Zeke is not?" Marie said softly, giving the dog a pat on the shoulder.

Mustard trotted up, nuzzling against Towser and smelling his backside. The two dogs ran circles again.

"Daniel, go and get some bacon from the wagon," Marie said. "Give Towser something to eat." She turned now to Jerry Bennett, mounted on his horse and moving the spare oxen along beside the wagons. "Mr. Bennett? What can it mean?"

She guessed that he could see the worry on her face. Maybe he gave an honest answer, or maybe he gave an answer that would give her a margin of comfort.

"Ma'am, I'd reckon that dog chased a coyote or a prairie dog or something, got separated from Mr. Zeke out here on the prairie. He's lucky to have found us. Maybe that's God's intervention. We busted an axle so that we'd come across Towser. I reckon Mr. Zeke is settin' down at Bridger's Fort right now, missing his old dog. Won't he be thrilled to see you again, and see that you've brought his dog to him?"

Marie nodded, fighting back the tears that seemed to rush to her eyes.

"Thank you, Mr. Bennett. What a kind and generous thought that is."

From his vantage some distance from the three wagons, Zeke watched the reunion of the two pals. He loved to see those dogs play together.

This was fine.

He was close enough to call to her. Close enough to see her bend over to pet the dog. Close enough to see that she and Daniel were well and whole. Close enough to protect her if it came to that.

This was fine.

29

THERE'D BEEN NO SIGN of Hubbard and his men. Jason Winter found the stop among the rocks where they'd camped two nights back, and the camp where the wagons had been when Elias sent him back.

He couldn't credit it, and said so to Jefferson Pilcher.

"I don't know how we never encountered that group of men."

"Maybe they went off hunting," Pilcher said. "Left the trail. Either way, Elias's concerns appear to have been unfounded."

Jason nodded his head, wishing he'd stayed with the main body of the wagon so that he could be with his wife now. He'd relished this journey, the time they'd been together. While the trek seemed to weigh on many of the other emigrants, for Jason it had been the best days of his life. Every day, walking beside Maggie. If they'd gone around the world like this for an eternity, it wouldn't have lasted long enough to suit him. While others spoke of tedious and tiring, Jason Winter could only think of every moment of this trip as wonderful.

But the last two days, riding alone at first and now with the three wagons, these had been hard days. Hard for being separated from Maggie, but hard, too, for the fear he had that he might soon find himself in a fight. The previous day had been worse – riding back to the east, all alone. He'd truly been scared that those men would pursue him, hoping to stop him from delivering his warning. And today, though he was surrounded by other people, he'd still found fear to be a constant companion – fear that an ambush might be hiding beyond the next rise.

But all that fear vanished after they reached the point of the encampments. Somehow, they'd not encountered those men. Jason rode foward, scouting the territory ahead, and when he came to the final crossing of the Sweetwater River, he turned and rode back to the three wagons.

"We're approaching the crossing for the Sweetwater," Jason announced, mostly to Caleb Driscoll, but also to anyone else who cared to hear. "About a mile up ahead."

"Late in the day for a river crossing," Jeff Pilcher said, walking forward from his own wagon.

"I'd rather start the morning on the far side of the river," Jerry Bennett offered. "My preference, when I have the choice, is to not start the day with water in my boots."

"It's an easy crossing," Jason said. "Might be complicated a bit by having a wagon on skids, but the trail runs right down the banks and through the river, and the river's no deeper than your knees. I'd suggest Mr. Weiss's wagon and Mr. Pilcher's go across first. Miss Marie's wagon last."

Pilcher shrugged his shoulders.

"If it's that simple of a crossing, then I'd agree that it would be better to get it done and out of the way. Start new tomorrow," he said.

"We shouldn't even have to unload anything, except for maybe with Miss Marie's wagon."

"It's decided then," Pilcher said.

As they approached the crossing, Caleb Driscoll climbed into the front of the Weiss wagon so that he could be inside for the crossing. Gabe Townes was already in Marie's wagon, but he pulled the oxen to a halt well short of the crossing to let Pilcher go through.

Jerry Bennett stopped the oxen and kept them corralled, intending to take them across when the wagons had all gone. Mrs. Weiss took off her shoes and Marcus Weiss removed his boots. He rolled his pants legs up to above his knees.

The water flowing down out of the Wind Mountains was cool, and as Marie waded through it, she dipped a hand into the water and pressed it against her face. Daniel had not just removed his shoes, but he also stripped out of his shirt and pants, and in the water he dunked himself all the way under. Marie let out a yelp and dropped her skirt to grab Daniel by the arm and pull him up. He was laughing as he came up, and Marie's skirt was soaked from the knees down.

Mrs. Pilcher and her three children waded across the river with similar mishap.

Jason rode across in front of the wagons, and Caleb Driscoll started across with Weiss's wagon. The crossing was a simple thing, like driving a team through a puddle. The current didn't shift the wagon at all. He topped the western bank without a problem and kept the wagon moving on past the women and children who had stopped to put their clothes back on.

Jeff Pilcher started down the eastern bank, the slope like a ramp right into the river.

And that's when the first shot came.

It was well-fired and struck Jason Winter's horse right in the head. The horse bolted, making it five yards, and then it kicked once and fell over dead. Jason could do no more than just hang tight to the reins, thinking at first that the shot had spooked the horse. He didn't even understand yet that it had been a shot. He'd just heard something and then his horse was running. The chaos of the moment disguised from him the true nature of the danger.

But when the horse fell dead, Jason found his leg pinned beneath it.

Jason heard one of the women scream.

The Sweetwater River flowed south from the Winds before it cut east. The last water to do so. All the other water west of the Sweetwater, it would make its way to the Pacific Ocean.

The Pacific.

It sounded as far away and exotic to Zeke Townes as China or Russia.

The emigrant trail crossed the river just above where it made its dramatic bend to the east. The river cut a fairly wide and shallow valley here, littered with scrub vegetation, squat juniper and other brush. And on either side of that valley, there were rolling hills. Not big hills, certainly, but the crossing was one of the few places where a man could look this way and that and realize that he was on a steady grade leading up to the South Pass.

Zeke hadn't really noticed it the two other times he'd come through here – first by himself, banished, and the second time going back east looking to warn his family.

He'd kept an eye on the wagons, traveling parallel to them, and far to the north. He was never more than two or maybe three miles from them, but he stayed behind hills or down in hollows, usually riding just a little behind so that he could see them but they would be hard pressed to see him. As they approached the river crossing, Zeke realized they had never crossed paths with Hubbard and his men.

He couldn't explain it. How had they missed each other?

The only explanation that Zeke could come up with was that Hubbard and his men abandoned the trail, perhaps fearing that they were being pursued by the men from the camp they'd attacked.

As the wagons prepared for the crossing, Zeke rode down into the underbrush in the river valley. He couldn't see the wagons now, but he could hear the laughter of children carrying across the prairie, and he could imagine how they were playing in the river to the chagrin of their mothers. At one point, he could have sworn that he heard Marie's soft voice call out, "Daniel!" followed by his son's laughter.

Hearing them proved better food than beefsteak; better medicine than laudanum.

Being in proximity to his family, Zeke felt fully restored. No hunger in his belly. No throbbing in his head. His arms felt strong. He didn't even mind the sun against his face.

The river made a bend just before the crossing, and that bend allowed Zeke to find a spot and ford the river without being seen by the folks down with the wagons. He got to the Western bank with the bay just behind, but he stayed down among the vegetation, keeping himself hidden. He guessed that Marie was also on the western bank of the river, now.

He wanted desperately to get to a vantage where he could see his wife and son, but he could not give himself away without risking the penalty of returning to the wagon train.

And then he heard Caleb Driscoll's voice give a shout to his oxen team. He heard one of the cows bellow and the rattle and clang as the wagon began to roll. A splash as the oxen entered the river.

He was so close to them, now.

Zeke heard the rifle shot.

He did not mistake. He did not question what had happened. He heard a woman scream from down river.

"Get up!" he called to Duke, and the gray lurched forward, through the underbrush at a gallop. The bay right behind.

They cleared the vegetation of the valley and sprang up an embankment, and Zeke was on high ground wheeling his horse toward the trail's crossing. He saw it now. Four mounted men on this side of the river. Six on the opposite side. It was Hubbard and his men. They were charging the emigrants – Zeke's family. A horse was down at the crossing.

Zeke slid his rifle from its scabbard. He had a load in the rifle. He fetched a cap from the box on his belt. His fingers seemed too big for the job, but he seated the cap, cocked the hammer to a full cock, and put the butt of his rifle against his shoulder.

One good shot, and he'd charge.

He took his aim at one of the riders charging in on his family. Moved the rifle to lead the man. Let out his breath. Squeezed the trigger. The hammer fell and the big rifle jerked. The recoil immediately reminded him of the bruises on his arms and chest, the pounding in his head.

"Damn!"

Zeke gritted his teeth. He'd missed his shot.

He pushed the rifle into its scabbard and called to Duke, giving the horse a tap with the heels from both feet. He didn't even hold the reins. They were just tucked down in his lap now. The horse sensed his excitement and bolted into the charge. Zeke grabbed his holster with one hand, the grip of his holster gun with the other. His hair sailed in the wind caused by the horse's gallop. He pulled the gun free from its leather and thumbed back the hammer, releasing the trigger.

He was going to hit the crossing about the same time as the four riders. He could see their blades in their hands. They intended to dismount and set upon their victims with knives.

One of those charging the people at the crossing – the one he'd shot at – had seen him now and wheeled his horse. Coming to intercept him. Zeke leaned forward, his face almost in Duke's mane. He kept the saddle gun low, almost pressed against Duke's shoulder. The man raised up his knife, ready to slash at Zeke. The silver blade glinting in the light from the setting sun.

Zeke sat up straight at the last moment, brought up the revolver. They were close enough to smell each other. Zeke pulled the trigger and the ball plunged into the chest of his adversary. The knife fell away. The man doubled over, his face going to his horse's mane.

Zeke didn't look back. He cocked the hammer and made for the next man.

The three of them were nearly up to the women and children. It looked like Jason Winter on the ground there, trapped beneath a fallen horse.

The three riders were reining in their horses now. One of them dropped from his saddle right over Jason Winter. The other two men didn't even seem to know that Zeke was there, but the one who'd set his sights on Jace, he looked back, saw Zeke.

A moment of indecision. Twenty yards to get into the fight.

Jason was already murdered if Zeke went for the two men now on foot and running toward his family. But if he went for Jason, he could save his niece's new husband. But at what risk to Marie and Daniel? Could he get to them in time?

And then he heard the screams, and Zeke's blood ran cold.

30

THEY WERE THE SAME Shoshone braves who had attacked Zeke.

There weren't but a score of them, but in that moment Zeke thought there must have been thousands. Their voices raised in a terrible war cry, the same war cry that Zeke had heard when they rushed him. The same cry that he knew would haunt his nightmares as long as he lived.

They must have been hiding down among the juniper and brush in the river's valley. Some of them, including one wearing Zeke's hat, so close to the emigrants they almost could have reached out and touched them when they made the river crossing.

Zeke drew reins, maybe from fear.

But as Duke stopped his charge and reared back a bit, Zeke turned on the man standing over Jason Winter. He aimed the saddle gun and dropped the hammer, and the man bent double as the lead ball burst into his gut.

"I can't stop to help," Zeke said to Jason. "Do your best to free yourself."

Jason's free foot was planted in the saddle as he tried to pry his stuck leg free. Leg was likely broke, Zeke figured, and the boy would be damned lucky to get clear of this with his hair on.

Zeke had no idea what to make of the sudden appearance of the Indians. He only knew to get to his family to protect them from wherever danger came. He swung his leg over Duke's neck and spun himself from the saddle. He grabbed at the bay's harness to steady the horse. He pulled the saddle gun and the rifle from the pannier's straps and now ran toward his wife and son.

Hubbard's men had no lingering question about where their priorities were.

The moment the Shoshone came out from cover, Hubbard's men turned away from the helpless victims to engage the new threat.

It all came on so fast, not a man among the three-wagon train had even armed himself. But Caleb Driscoll now hopped down from the lead wagon. He drew a heavy-bladed knife from his belt and shouted to the women and children.

"Here! Come to the wagon!"

In that same moment, Marie saw Zeke. Their eyes locked. Daniel clutching to her waist, her with both hands on her son's shoulders. He could see the terror in her face.

"Go to Caleb!" Zeke shouted to her.

Just then, a Shoshone man leapt between them, a hatchet in his fist, and he fell into hand-to-hand combat with one of Hubbard's men.

The white man plunged a knife into the gut of the Indian, and then he swung it up again. The Indian fell away.

Zeke stood motionless, uncertain where he fit in this fight.

Should he turn against the Shoshone who were killing the men who'd intended to kill his family? Was it white men against Indians and the Shoshone against all?

But on the far bank, Zeke saw Hubbard. Hubbard and the five over there were still mounted. A couple of them, Hubbard included, had drawn rifles. Others had long knives and were slashing at the Indians who had appeared around them. Though the Shoshone clearly had the advantage in numbers, Hubbard and his men looked presently like they would win the day on the far side of the river.

All around was absolute chaos.

Mrs. Pilcher was screaming. She'd dropped to her knees, wrapping up the youngest of her children in her arms and covering the child with her body. But she was screaming as if that would protect them. Marie had Daniel in her arms, and she'd pulled him back to the wagon. She was standing with her back to the wagon and Caleb Driscoll, knife in hand, standing in front of her. He seemed as reluctant as Zeke felt to get into the fight.

Towser and Mustard and the other dogs, they were all running around, barking – insane with the havoc. Everything was noise and confusion, and Zeke's entire concept of the world had shrunk to maybe thirty square yards right around this river crossing. He didn't know anything of the Platte or the Devil's Gate or Bridger's Fort. All of life was lived in this small space and this brief moment.

The other Pilcher children were back at the wagon, too. And there was Gabe, Zeke's nephew. He was still on the far bank. Jerry Bennett was with him, both of them had knives in their hands. They had their backs to one of the wagons and looked ready to defend themselves. Jeff Pilcher was in the bed of his wagon, the oxen standing on the west bank, the wagon in the river. Pilcher was standing up, now, a rifle to his shoulder. He was looking for a target to shoot at, but didn't seem to know what to shoot at or who to kill.

Hubbard's men were fighting with the Indians, and it was a terrible struggle. Shoshone braves running at them, Hubbard's men slashing with their knives or swinging rifle butts like clubs.

Hubbard himself was still mounted, a rifle in his hands.

Even as Zeke watched, Hubbard's rifle burst into a cloud of smoke, and a Shoshone man who'd charged him fell dead on the bank of the river. Hubbard started to reload his rifle.

One thing Zeke knew for certain, it was Hubbard and the other men in his company who had first charged Marie and the others. Whatever else was happening here at the river crossing leading into the South Pass, it was Hubbard and his men who came here to kill Zeke Townes's family.

Zeke had one saddle gun tucked into his belt and his rifle in his left hand. The other saddle gun was in his right fist. Now he shoved it into his belt, too. He plucked a cap from the box on his belt and fit it into place on the rifle. He raised the rifle and found Johnny Hubbard on the other end of the barrel.

He pulled the trigger. A burst of white smoke. And when the wind whipped it away, Hubbard dropped his rifle and looked around.

Their eyes met, Zeke and Hubbard.

A Shoshone brave grabbed Hubbard by the arm and wrenched him from the saddle.

"Caleb Driscoll!" Zeke shouted, trying desperately to be heard over the din of the shrieks and shouts. Dogs were barking and snarling, and even as he watched, Zeke saw one of the Shoshone bash one of his dogs with a hatchet. "Get that damned wagon rolling!"

One thought kept going through Zeke's mind: We must leave this; we must get away from here.

The nature of the attack, coming from both banks in the middle of a river crossing, had left them trapped. They had to move.

Hubbard's two men on this side of the bank were putting up a hell of a fight.

Zeke could see three Shoshone men on the ground, dead or dying. Another now tried a swipe with a spear, but one of those two white men caught the spear between his arm and ribs and jerked it free of the Shoshone's grip. Now he set on the weaponless man with his knife, tossing the spear aside. Zeke ran at the man, wielding his rifle like a club. He swung it down hard on the man's back, and he fell away from the Shoshone.

Caleb was slapping one of the oxen, shouting and calling to it, but the beast didn't move. Finally, Caleb grabbed the harness and heaved, and the oxen started to go.

But with the wagon moving, Marie and Daniel had no cover. She'd gathered up the two other Pilcher children in her arms, and she was pushing all of them with the wagon. Caleb Driscoll shouted at the oxen, slapped their rumps. Anything to get them moving.

A Shoshone brave took a swing at Zeke and nearly brained him. The hatchet caught him on the shoulder, and left a bloody cut through shirt and skin. It was the one who'd stolen his hat. They took two things from him, his rope and his hat.

Zeke used the rifle butt like a ram and pushed the Indian back. The man lost his footing on a rock and tumbled backwards.

He tossed the rifle aside and stepped over to Mrs. Pilcher, who was still screaming and covering her child. Zeke grabbed the woman by her shoulders and lifted her off the ground so that she was standing. She screamed in his face and, having lost her child, occupied her fists in punching at Zeke's chest.

"Mrs. Pilcher!" Zeke shouted at her. "Get ahold to yourself. Help Marie gather your children. Get moving away from here!"

Still, she screamed and punched, so Zeke slapped her across the face.

"Save your children, woman!" he shouted at her.

"Mr. Townes?" she said, recognizing him for the first time.

"Collect your children. Run from here!"

The wagon was going now. It would be up even with Zeke and the Pilcher woman in a few moments. Marie and Mrs. Weiss had Daniel and the two Pilcher children corralled, and they were crouched low, moving along with the wagon. Caleb had fetched the whip from the wagon and was swinging it wildly over the oxen, shouting to them.

Mrs. Pilcher looked at them and rushed the few feet to the wagon, grabbing one of her children by the hand and pulling the child along. But she'd left the one on the ground, now at Zeke's feet. So he grabbed the child and pulled him to his feet and pushed him toward the other children and the three women.

Caleb looked at Zeke in that moment, his face strained with fear and worry.

"Just keep them moving, Caleb," Zeke said. "You must leave this."

Caleb nodded his head.

Mustard had gone near to Marie and Daniel, snarling and barking but staying close to the family. He was all teeth and spit, and if Zeke was a Shoshone, he might think twice about trying against that dog. Towser was always close to Zeke, barking and snarling and adding to the din and confusion in the moment. Twice, or three times, Towser jumped at Zeke's back, planting his front two paws square onto Zeke, but not knocking him off balance. One of the times, was when Zeke used his rifle butt to knock down the Shoshone brave who'd stoled his hat.

Pilcher did not need to be told to move his wagon. As soon as the Weiss wagon began to move, Pilcher's oxen followed. They nearly dumped him as the wagon lurched forward.

Hubbard's two men, still fighting the Indians on this bank, had moved instinctively toward the river, toward the others of their outfit. Zeke recognized one of them now, knew him by name. It was Winthrop, the one who'd showed him the pole with the scalps. As Pilcher's wagon came up out of the river and moved on behind the Weiss's wagon, the fighting centered right there beside the river.

Winthrop and the other man were slashing with their knives, desperately engaged with four or five of the Shoshone.

Across the bank, Zeke saw an Indian straddling Hubbard while he removed the man's scalp. Hubbard kicked his legs and screamed, but couldn't get free. Scalped while still alive.

"We've got to get out of here," Zeke shouted.

Jerry Bennett was mounted now, and he'd ridden up to the oxen pulling Zeke's wagon with the skids. Jerry had hold of the lead ox's harness, and Zeke's nephew had returned to the wagon, whip in hand. But the oxen wouldn't go farther than the edge of the water for the men fighting on this bank.

Zeke drew both of the saddle guns from his belt and rushed toward the river's edge. He thumbed back the hammers on both of the big guns. As he reached the fighting, Winthrop and the other man were fending off the Indians. The six or seven of them doing a kind of war dance, all crouched and facing each other.

Zeke shouldered one of the Indians out of the way, stretched out both arms, one gun pointing at Winthrop's gut and the other pointing at the second man's chest. He squeezed both triggers at the same moment.

The Shoshone braves fell on the two men like vultures, dragging them away from the river and scalping them. A couple of the Indians faced Zeke now, their hatchets clutched in their hands. He spun on them and cocked the hammers of the two saddle guns, extending them as an offer to violence.

"I am not your enemy!" Zeke shouted at the men. "Get away from me!"

The warriors backed away, having seen what those saddle guns did to Winthrop and the other man.

"I am not your friend, neither!" Zeke shouted. "You think I won't kill you after that beating you gave me?"

Gabe's oxen plunged into the river. Zeke kept the two Indians at bay.

Zeke's wagon, on skids, mired in the river. But Gabe worked that whip and shouted, and the oxen dug in, and the wagon pulled clear. They should have run that busted wagon through first, before the riverbed and the bank were all mushed by the first oxen, but Gabe had made it now. As the wagon climbed the slope, Gabe dropped from the front and ran ahead to where Jason Winter remained trapped and struggled against the weight of his horse pressing down on him. Gabe drew the long rifle from Jason's saddle and wedged it under the horse, beside Jason's leg. Then he used the rifle like a lever, getting just enough lift that Jason was able to slide his leg out.

Maggie's younger brother helped her husband to his feet. Zeke glanced back and saw Jason limping toward the wagon, in obvious discomfort. But maybe the leg wasn't broken.

At the same time, Jerry Bennett started to cross the river, but then he drew reins and looked back at the spare oxen. There were a couple of steers, a couple of spare horses, and enough oxen to provide a second team for each of the three wagons.

"The livestock!" Jerry shouted to Zeke, and started to wheel his horse to go back.

"Hell on those cows!" Zeke shouted back, not taking his eyes off the Indians. "You leave 'em, Jerry! Get these people out of here!"

Jerry Bennett turned his horse west and dashed through the river. Coming even with Zeke, he reined in. His horse dancing, skittish in the excitement with the smell of blood and gunpowder hanging in the air.

"Come on," Jerry said. "Mount up, Mr. Zeke. Let's go."

"I'll cover your retreat," Zeke said, though the wagons were moving forward and not back. "You keep them all moving!"

Zeke Townes lifted the barrels of the saddle guns toward the air and took a couple of tentative steps back, away from the two Shoshone men.

The fight had shifted entirely to the other side of the river.

Hubbard's men were finished, now. As he glanced beyond the two Shoshone warriors, Zeke saw two Indians holding one of Hubbard's men under the water of the river. Beyond them, an Indian was removing the scalp of another of Hubbard's men. Only three still stood on their feet down near the river, and they were on the verge of being overwhelmed. One of them had a rifle loaded. He was using it to hold off four of the Shoshone. One of them approached, tried to grab the barrel of the rifle, and the man pulled the trigger. The Indian fell back, but the others set upon Hubbard's man.

Two still on their feet.

One of those two was shouting to Zeke, begging him for help.

Zeke took a couple more steps back. The two Indians he'd held at gunpoint now turned, wanting to get into the last of the fight before it was over. Zeke turned, too, running back over the ground he'd fought through moments before. He found his rifle still on the ground and lifted it up. Then he found the other rifle. He checked back over his shoulder. None of the Indians were coming in pursuit.

Duke and the bay had started to follow the wagons and were some distance away now, so Zeke stopped and turned to face the river. He loaded first one of the rifles and then the other.

With the saddle guns tucked into his belt and a rifle in each hand, Zeke started in the wake of the wagons. He twisted around to keep his eyes on his backtrail while he walked toward the wagons or turned and walked backwards.

The oxen dragged those wagons painfully slow, and the last wagon – Zeke's wagon – went even slower. But they cleared the river by a hundred yards or more, and Zeke had caught up to them by now. There, Marcus Weiss came out from behind a rise. He'd run. Zeke didn't know if he'd run when Hubbard's men turned up or if he made his escape when the Shoshone attacked. It didn't much matter. He'd run to get himself clear of the fighting while his three young children huddled in the wagon and his wife endured the battle with the other women. He'd shown himself for a coward, and though no one said anything to him, all the emigrants watched him as he sulked back into their company.

Jerry Bennett rode back a little ways to meet Zeke.

"Mr. Zeke, I'm damned proud to see you," Jerry said. "I reckon you just about saved us."

"Those Shoshone saved us," Zeke said. "Though if we'd stayed around, who can say what they'd have done with us."

Jerry looked down toward the river.

"They ain't coming after us," he said.

"That doesn't mean they won't," Zeke said. "We've got to keep these people moving."

Jerry looked ahead at the setting sun.

"Be dark in an hour and a half or two hours," Jerry said.

"Keep 'em moving, Jerry. As long as we can. We'll have to camp tight tonight and be prepared for those Indians to come at us in the dark. Won't be much sleep for those of us on watch."

Jerry chuckled.

"Be a sleepless night for all of us, I reckon."

"Likely so," Zeke agreed.

They'd caught up to the wagons now, walking as they talked.

"I'll let Caleb know not to slow down, though I doubt he'll have to be told," Jerry said, giving his horse a slight touch with his knee.

Weiss had come into the wagon train at the front, but he wasn't walking along. Instead, he stood rooted to the ground as Jeff Pilcher's wagon passed him. Now he raised a finger at Zeke.

"You've been banished from this wagon train, sir!" Marcus Weiss shouted. "You know the punishment for a banished man who returns."

Weiss had shamed himself, abandoning his wife and children and running for the hills. Now he saw opportunity to shift focus away from him and onto Zeke. Or anyhow, that's how Zeke saw it.

"Hush, you!" Marie Townes said, turning on Marcus Weiss. She was up near the front wagon – Weiss's wagon. She had Daniel and the Pilcher children in front of her, along with Pilcher's wife. "My husband has saved your miserable life!"

Jerry Bennett tugged reins and stepped his horse right at Weiss, as if he intended to knock the man down.

"You listen to me," Jerry growled. "You say one more word about banishment, I'll put you down myself. This man saved your life."

Jeff Pilcher now advanced on Marcus Weiss. He'd felt his own responsibility in Zeke's sending off. His wife was among the most vocal of the women who said they would not continue on with a murderer among their party. But didn't she now appreciate the man? Didn't she now appreciate a man who could turn to violence?

God knew, Jeff Pilcher appreciated Zeke Townes. He'd seen one of those other men, dragged to the ground by three or four of those savage bastards, his hair cut from his skull as he screamed and thrashed. That would have been the fate of all of them, the men, the women, and the children. Pilcher didn't doubt it.

Zeke Townes had come in like thunder on the wind, those saddle guns spitting fire. He'd, halted Hubbard's men, delayed the Indian attack, cleared a path, and gotten the wagons moving. Pilcher was firm in his certainty that if Zeke hadn't turned up when he did, right at this moment, he'd be watching his wife and children fall under the knives of those Indians.

"Belay that tongue!" Pilcher swore at Marcus Weiss. "Another word from you, and it'll be I who banishes you from this wagon train!"

Caleb Driscoll had stopped walking alongside the Weiss's wagon, turning to watch what was happening with the other men. Gabe had stopped, too. The oxen were still going, but their pace was beginning to slow. Behind them, the fighting had stopped. It was all done now back at the crossing. The Shoshone had completed their revenge. What Zeke didn't know was if they'd be satisfied, or if they would turn their vengeance on every white face they saw.

"Enough of all this," Zeke said. "If I have to face a trial, I'll do it at Bridger's Fort. For now, we've got to keep moving, and get ourselves organized for a defense should we have to make a stand against those Indians. You men see to your rifles, load them, but do not cap them. Be sure of your knives and your percussion caps. Collect your families and be ready to defend them. Mr. Bennett, get back on your horse and watch our backtrail, please. Caleb, keep those damned oxes marching!"

They all had their dander up, all those men. The excitement of the moment coursed through them. Their hearts were pounding, their blood rushing. It would be an easy enough thing to start throwing punches among themselves, but that wasn't what was called for now.

Zeke hadn't hardly even seen her coming, but suddenly Marie threw herself into his arms. He still had those rifles in his hands as he caught her. She squeezed him, both arms around him. And then Daniel was there, arms wrapped around Zeke's waist.

"I'm glad to see you," Zeke said, holding onto his wife as best he could with those long rifles in his hands.

"You look terrible," Marie said with a laugh, and her laughter quickly turned to tears.

Just before night, they stopped the wagons. They'd gone fewer than three miles, certainly. Maybe only two. The oxen pulling those wagons were slow moving beasts.

They pulled the wagons into a circle as best they could and used rope to create a corral that would keep the remaining oxen inside that circle.

Gabe and Caleb did most of the work with the animals. Jeff Pilcher and Marcus Weiss stayed with the women and children. Both men stood armed with rifles and knives, but Pilcher doubted that Weiss would stay nearby if trouble came. Zeke had told Pilcher, if it comes to it, tell them all to run. Scatter. Maybe some of them will survive. Jefferson Pilcher tightened his grip on his rifle, intending that it would not come to that, not as long as he had breath in his body.

They'd made a pallet for Jason Winter under one of the wagons, and Zeke had left him with Elias's saddle gun.

Jerry Bennett stood watch with Zeke.

The two of them rode circles around the wagons, watching in the dim light for any movement. Sometimes they rode together, sometimes they rode in opposite directions.

No one slept.

It would be harder going now. A four or five day ride to Bridger's Fort would turn into eight or ten days. Probably, some company of men from the fort would ride back to check on them on the eighth day. Elias and some of the others. Zeke hoped they'd be alive to greet them.

31

—— • ——

"If a body of emigrants could limp into this fort, I'd say you're limping." Bearded, with a weather-beaten complexion and sandy hair, the thin faced man met the travelers several hundred yards from the fort. Zeke rode out front of the wagons on the gray horse. Daniel rode a little ways behind him on the bay, his legs too short to get his feet in the stirrups.

"Limping or not, I'm just glad to have arrived," Zeke said, bending over and extending a hand to the man.

"I'm Jim Bridger, folks call me Old Gabe. Welcome!"

Zeke nodded his thanks and looked out at the fort. A rectangular log compound consisting of a dozen buildings forming a large courtyard and a log stockade beside it, the place wasn't particularly impressive. Maybe a score of Indian lodges made of hide were set up out in front of the place, and there were dozens of white men and women, black men, and Indians alike. Most of them were just milling around outside of the fort, but some were engaged in games while it seemed that others were conducting business of one kind or another. Some folks hauled armloads of supplies out of the fort and toward their wagons. Off to one side, Zeke saw his brother's wagon train, but it was not the only one there. There must have been two or three full wagon trains. Scores of mules and oxen, water barrels and cracker boxes stacked everywhere.

After weeks of moving through the fresh air, Zeke's first sense of Bridger's Fort – other than the sight of it – was the stench that reached his nostrils.

"You can't imagine how much we've looked forward to getting here," Zeke said.

"I've got some idea," Bridger told him. "You've been the cause of much discussion and excitement around here. I'm eager for you to tell me what occurred with Hubbard and those men."

Zeke swung a leg and dropped down out of the saddle. He walked to the bay and lifted Daniel down.

"Run along to your mama now, son," Zeke said.

Elias and Henry Blair and some of the other men had come back a couple of days ago, searching for the three wagons. They'd made it in time to help with the crossing at the Green River, an affair most emigrants found exceedingly more difficult than the final crossing of the Sweetwater, though Ezekiel Townes would never remember it that way.

"You deal with all sorts out here," Bridger said, almost by way of apology. "Some are more honest than others. It's rough country, and if I wasn't willing to trade with rough men, I'd never be able to survive at this place."

"I reckon so," Zeke said. He didn't blame Bridger for Hubbard's actions.

When they'd accomplished the crossing, Elias and the other men rode back to Bridger's, so the story of Hubbard's attack and the Shoshone attack had already spread among all the people at Bridger's Fort.

"I reckon Hubbard knew of these three wagons and thought they'd be easy prey," Zeke said to Bridger. "But those Shoshone were looking for Hubbard, and when he attacked, they attacked as well."

"It was an ambush of the ambush," Bridger said.

"That's exactly what it was. I can't say where those Indians came from. If they'd been lying in wait at the crossing, or if they'd just come up. Either way, it was an exciting affair."

Bridger grinned.

"I imagine it was," he said. "You'll find these parts are full of excitement."

Elias was approaching now, along with some others from the wagon train. Friends coming to greet friends. Especially a few of the women from the wagon train came out to greet the other women. Elias embraced his younger brother and clapped him on the back. Maggie came rushing out to find her new husband, now with his leg in a splint in the back of her uncle's wagon.

"It is good to see you here," Elias said.

"It is good to be here."

Zeke plucked his hat from his head and ran his sleeve across his brow.

When he'd come out to meet the three wagons at the Green River, Elias had brought with him a new hat for Zeke, purchased at Bridger's Fort. It was a black hat with a low crown and a wide brim, and Zeke saw now that it was the exact sort of hat that Bridger himself wore. Elias had also relieved Zeke's conscience at the Green River when he informed his younger brother that the main body of the wagon train came across Zeke's pack on the trail – the one he'd tossed from the bay's back during his night walk. The sack of coins was in the pack, Elias told him.

"I know you need to rest," Elias said. "But there won't be much time for it. Mr. Bridger has said we're traveling so late that we need to make haste to Oregon City and through the Blue Mountains before snows come, but he thinks we can do it. You and the others rest yourselves today and tomorrow. We'll take care of repairing your axle. But day after tomorrow, we'll all set out together."

"What about my banishment?" Zeke asked.

"I've talked to the others. I've told them that I'm going on with you, and if anyone wants to join the two of us, they're welcome. If they refuse to travel with you, then they can stay here or go back for all I care. Every wagon in this train will go with you, Zeke. They all heard what you did, riding back and saving the others. All is forgiven, Zeke. At least as far as these folks are concerned."

"Marcus Weiss may not be so forgiving," Zeke said.

"Hell on him," Elias muttered. "He'll be forgiving if he chooses to continue to travel with us, and there's a couple of other wagon trains here if he doesn't care to. One of them is bound for California if he'd rather go that way and avoid ever seeing you again."

Zeke nodded his head.

"That would be fine with me."

"It's a rough trail ahead, but I've found a group of men – seven of them – who are packing to Oregon City. They'd like to travel with us, and their buy-in is their labor on the trail. They're freighters, familiar with this area. Done business with Mr. Bridger before. I'll introduce you to Neil Rimmer tomorrow."

"Great," Zeke said. "A bath, a good night's sleep, maybe a meal or two. I'll be ready to leave out for Oregon City day after tomorrow."

AFTERWORD

Dear Reader,

Thank you so much for riding along with the Townes Party through the South Pass. I hope you enjoyed the journey!

But the trip is hardly over for Zeke and Marie, Elias, Captain Walker and the other members of the the Townes party.

The hardest part of the trail still lies ahead for them. West of Bridger's Fort, the trail becomes far more treacherous. The river crossings and steep cliff faces and the threat of early snows all loom ahead of the emigrants. And ahead, there are fewer forts, fewer people, fewer opportunities for salvation.

And Neil Rimmer has hired on as guide.

Don't miss "To the Green Valleys Yonder," the second book of the Townes Party on the Oregon Trail series.

Sincerely,
Robert Peecher

ALSO BY

If you love traditional Westerns, I'd encourage you to check out my Robert Peecher author page on Amazon.

If you've never read any of my Westerns before but you're interested, I would encourage you to take a look at these books:

"Too Long the Winter" – a short, standalone novel that's a great example of my Westerns.

"Bred in the Bone" – The first book in the Heck & Early series.

"Rankin's Posse" – The first book in the Marshal from Ocate Trilogy.

"Blood on the Mountain" – The first book in the Moses Calhoun Trilogy.

All of these and more can be found on the Robert Peecher author page on Amazon.

ALSO BY

While I'm mostly known for writing traditional Westerns, I do sometimes dabble in other genres. If you're a fan of modern mysteries and thrillers, I hope you'll check out my novel "Under the Dixie Moon."

It's deep-fried Southern justice when an investigator returns to his small town roots to take on a corrupt sheriff and the Dixie Mafia. If you love stories of down-home murder up in the hills of Dixie, small-town criminals, and deep-fried Southern justice, then slide into the passenger seat of this '67 Camaro and buckle up. You might want to wear a cowboy hat, and you'd better bring along your Colt Python, because what gets buried Under the Dixie Moon always comes back up.

Click here to grab a copy today!

ABOUT AUTHOR

Robert Peecher is the author of more than 60 novels. He's an avid outdoorsman and loves paddling rivers and hiking trails. He lives in Georgia with his wife Jean. You can follow him on Facebook at Robert Peecher Author.